THE FAT MASCOT

22 Wildly Funny Baseball Stories (and more!)

BY

ROBERT RUDD WHITING.

Illustrated by the Author

Jacket Art — Mark Ritterbush

Lincoln-Herndon Press, Inc.
818 South Dirksen Parkway
Springfield, IL 62703

THE FAT MASCOT
22 Wildly Funny Baseball Stories and More!

Second Edition

Manufactured in the United States of America.

For information write:

The Lincoln-Herndon Press, Inc.
818 South Dirksen Parkway
Springfield, Illinois 62703

Library of Congress Cataloguing in Publication Data.
Library of Congress Catalogue Card Number: 87-082709
ISBN 0-942936-14-0 (Softcover)

CONTENTS.

1.

CONTENTS.

II.

ACKNOWLEDGEMENTS

We are grateful to the following individuals and institutions for information about Robert Rudd Whiting.

Earl E. Coleman
University Archivist, Princeton University
Princeton, NJ

Robin McElheny
Curatorial Assistant for the Visual Collection
Harvard University
Cambridge, MA

Denis R. Tippo
Director of Alumni and Parent Affairs
Phillips Academy
Andover, MA

Larry Weyhrich
Reference Librarian
Illinois State Library
Springfield, IL

INTRODUCTION

Robert Rudd Whiting, the author of these unique baseball tall tales, was born in New York in 1877. He came from typical upper-class and affluent parents who sent him to the best schools—Andover Academy, then on to Harvard University. He finished his last two years of academic training at Princeton University.

After college, he began his life-long profession of journalism with five years on the **New York Sun**. His final work was as the editor of **Ainsley's Magazine**. But the last year of his life was spent as the volunteer Assistant Director of the Committee On Public Affairs, during World War I. While serving his country, he became ill with the influenza that was then an epidemic threatening the entire nation, and died of it.

Whiting was a literary man all of his life, writing articles, novels and short stories, almost all reflecting the upper-class, cultured and affluent standards and style of his own life. And this makes it all the more curious when we know that his most enduring work was in the tall tale genre, his wildly humorous whoppers that seemed more typical of rural and lower-class writers—writers for "down home" folks—or so it seemed to the critics of that time. But Whiting was a master at this unlikely form of typical American humor not at all indulged in by the literary and fashionable writers of his day. It is, therefore, easy to understand that one literary critic could label his last book of tall tales "absurd". It is also easy to suppose that Whiting thumbed his nose at the critic and said, "Well! Of course it's absurd. But so are our mountains absurdly high. And our rivers absurdly long. And our cities absurdly large, to say nothing of our absurdly rich prairies. America is so "teetotaciously" unique that "absurd" is, perhaps, not strong enough to describe it...or my tall tales that try to put the wonder of it all in understandable terms. Thanks for the compliment!"

Whiting's natural talent for writing tall tales was given impetus and material by the wonderful inventions of his time. One biographer said of his work: "There was no invention mentioned in the news column of the day, from gas engines to liquid air, that Whiting did not use in his stories."

The literary men of the latter part of the last century and early in this one tended to ape British humor, the quiet, literary, subtle humor that evoked a gentle laugh or smile. But, curiously, that kind of humor did not interest Whiting. He wrote in the robust style loved by the average American about whom Andrew Lang wrote, in the last half of the 18th century, "All over the land of America men are eternally swapping stories at bars, and in the long endless journeys by railway and steamer. How little, comparatively, the English 'swap stories'." And the fun in traditional "story-swapping", is evidenced in these 31 stories. It is as if we were sitting around our den or at a bar, listening to Bob Whiting tell his stories... and exchanging stories with him.

Scholars once thought that the whopper, the windy... the tall tale, was a frontier form of humor. Today we know that the "whopper" delighted all Americans. And today, the tall tale is as popular as it was 100 years ago. The contents of some of the newspapers featured on the racks at supermarkets contain tall tales so wonderful, imaginative and professionally wrought that they stand beside our Paul Bunyan tales, and those of Mike Fink, Pecos Bill and Baron Munchhausen. Thus, Robert Rudd Whiting writes in the American tall tale tradition, the tradition of our poetic, imaginative and wildly funny story tellers, in all times. And if you doubt it, listen to Johnny Carson describe how hot it was. Or read in the **Illinois State Journal**, the contributions of readers who tell with tall stories just how hot it was in Springfield, Illinois. The tall story is with us today as it always was and will be. And Robert Rudd Whiting was a master story-teller in that tradition.

Now...on to the Lightfoot Lilies, the ball club of Oxendale, in Jones County, U.S.A.

"PLA-A-A-Y BALL!"

PRELIMINARIES.

The fat man sitting next to me on the bleachers leaned over between innings and whispered, "See that feller in front of you? Look at his hands. Baseball did that."

I looked at the man's hands. The skin was off his fingers, and they were badly bruised.

"What position does he play?" I whispered back.

"He never played."

"But his hands?"

"He hurt'em cheering at a deaf mutes' game."

That was my first conversation with the fat ex-mascot of the Lightfoot Lilies.

BASEBALL STORIES.

I.

THE FAT EX-MASCOT STOOPS TO CONQUER.

"I admit that I don't look much like an athlete," remarked the man, whose 320 pounds were mostly grouped beneath his waistcoat, "but I was the means of winning one of the hottest baseball games ever played. It was along in the '80's, when the Lightfoot Lilies and the Ringtail Roarers were rivals for the championship of Jones County. I was a tall man then—lying down. I was even stouter than I am now. So you can well imagine that I was ineligible as a regular lightfoot. I was a hot rooter for the team, however, and a great friend of Captain Slugger Burrows, so the boys allowed me to warm the bench during their trips as a sort of combination mascot and non-playing substitute, and I think you'll agree with me when I say it was lucky for them they did.

"It was the final game of the series that I did my star work in. The Roarers had won the first game through the phenomenal work of their pitcher, Cy Priest. We captured the second contest because Cy was up against it and couldn't play. Then came the great contest of which I'm going to tell you. The news spread before the game that Cy had missed the train and the Roarers would have to use their sub pitcher. Our crowd were simply wild with joy. The Lily band played music that would put a circus out of business, and my enthusiastic substituting was only overshadowed by the great work I did later on. But we didn't have such a cinch in spite of Cy Priest's absence. The game was played with varying fortunes, and at the end of the ninth the score was 32—32. The Roarers had gone to bat first and in their half of the tenth we held them down to three runs, thanks to Slugger Burrows' freezing on to a hot one with one hand at short.

"Then came our half, and things started off with a rush. Their twirler couldn't keep the pill over the pie, and the first two up drew free passes. Sam Strong singled, filling the bases. Then came Burrows with one of his old-time two-baggers that cleared the bases and the crowd went wild. Men smashed their hats, women wept with joy, the band kicked the bass drum, and, oh Lord, how I did mascot! The score was tied, and none out. When the next two men drew bases on balls, filling the bases again, our joy knew no limits. Like Monte Cristo, we thought we had the world by the neck.

"But right here something happened. Suddenly one of the Roarers' rooters stood up in his seat and pointed excitedly toward the road. Then the whole of their side of the grandstand jumped to their feet and yelled like people possessed. And they had reason to, for there was Cy Priest in a buggy driving like mad for the grounds. The excitement stopped the game right there until Cy pulled his horse up short in front of the grandstand. He got out and without a word walked straight toward the pitcher's box and peeled off his coat.

" 'Give me that ball,' he demanded, without a word of explanation. 'You can't pitch; go sit on the bench.'

"Well, sir, you'd be surprised to see the difference Cy Priest made in that game when things got going again. Bull Thompson popped up an easy one to third, and the three men on bases never budged an inch. Home Run Hankins was called out on strikes before he knew he was at the bat. Things were getting serious, for Captain Burrows saw that if we couldn't win this inning with three men on bases there would never be another chance while Cy was in the box. He called the players around him and after a moment's discussion dumfounded the crowd by calling 'Willie Little to the bat,' Willie Little being your humble servant.

"But there was method in his madness as was seen the minute I stepped in the batter's box. You see my corporation overlapped the plate by a foot or so, and in order not to force in a run on a dead ball or four wide ones, Cy had to pitch the ball over the plate in the small space opposite my neck or else just above my knees. As I might easily hit the ball if it came across my neck, and as such a thing was a physical impossibility if he placed it below my corporation, he decided upon the latter course. The first two he pitched were balls and the crowd laughed, although with me it was a most serious moment. Then came a strike, a ball and another strike in rapid succession, making it three balls and two strikes. The strain was intense, and even the band kept silent. Cy rubbed some dirt upon the ball and hitched his trousers. Slowly he swung his arm back and the next minute I saw the ball coming straight as a die across my knees. I had but a second to think, but I thought quickly. Bending my knees I caught the ball square in the stomach. 'Dead ball, take yer base!' yelled the umpire and the winning run was forced in. The Roarers protested that I had tried to get hit, but the umpire looked at me and shook his head. 'He didn't have to,' he said.

"My modesty forbids me describing the way the crowd bore me off the field upon their shoulders, and you can't realize what that means if you've never tried it. I will say, however, that that article in the *Jones County Courier* headed, 'He Stoops to Conquer,' was as complimentary a thing as I've ever read outside of an obituary notice."

II.

CATCHERS AND THEIR PECULIARITIES.

"There are a good many catchers in the base-ball business," the fat man who was formerly mascot for the Lightfoot Lilies remarked, "but have you ever noticed how few of them are really what you'd call stars? No matter how good a man may be behind the bat it seems he always has some fault that offsets his good qualities.

"Take Dinkey Dooley of the Lightfoot Lilies, for example. He was one of the best backstops that ever wore a muzzle, but his accursed foppishness caused his downfall. On more than one occasion he got into trouble with Dean Braley, the pitcher, because Braley, so he said, intentionally rubbed dirt on the ball before each delivery. Dooley's finish came one Fourth of July game against the Ringtail Roarers. It was the hottest day ever known in Jones County and Jones County is about the hottest place I know of excepting one. Everybody was peevish and out of sorts, but things ran along all right until the Roarers' half of the seventh. The bases were full, two were out, and the batter had three balls and two strikes called on him. Braley gave his trousers a hitch and was just about to pitch the ball when he noticed that Dooley was acting strangely. Dinkey was sniffing his nose in the air.

" 'What's the matter, hurt?" asked Captain Slugger Burrows, running in from short.

" 'Really, captain, you know I never could stand the smell of burning rubber, and—phew—I really think the sun is melting the home plate. Phew!'

"Now, wouldn't that scald you? They had to take the ice out of the oatmeal water and put it on the plate before Dinkey would consent to finish the game out. Well, as you can imagine, Slugger Burrows wasn't the man to stand for that sort of thing, and next day Dooley got his release.

"Foxey Flenner, the next catcher we tried, was all right while he lasted, but he came to grief through one of his own tricks. He had a habit of stretching his hands out in front of the plate and nabbing the ball before it reached the batter. That worked all right until one day he tried to gobble in a straight one that the batter had picked out for a home run. Foxey broke seven fingers, dislocated his right thumb, and was charged with an error by the scorer for dropping the ball. He seemed to lose his sand after that and soon quit the game for good.

"Bull Thompson was the next man to try for the position, and he turned out to be a wonder. He could stop anything from a cable car down with one hand; he always kept the ball on the carpet when he hit; his lamps were always lit when he was on base, while as for throwing to second he was the best ever. His one fault, when he first joined us, was his forgetfulness. He had the worst memory of any man I ever knew. Sometimes he used to forget to run after he had hit the ball, and we had to tie a string on his finger to make him remember. Once he forgot which way the bases went and ran to third instead of first. After that we tied two strings on his finger. But the worst of all was in one game with the Roarers when he tried to throw to second. He brought his arm forward with terrific force, but forgot to let go of the ball. It carried him clear off his feet, and he landed, face down, five yards in front of the plate. He nursed a broken nose for almost three weeks, and after that was able to remember without even the aid of strings.

"Every great artist seems to have some failing. Funny, isn't it? I suppose it's what they call the eccentricity of genius."

III.

DEAN BRALEY INVENTS THE AUTOMOROLLER SKATES

"It's odd," reflected the fat ex-mascot of the Lightfoot Lilies, "how all great inventive geniuses seem to be lazy men. I suppose it's because they're always trying to get next to some scheme for minimizing exertion. Now, there was old Dean Braley, who did the twirling for the Lightfoots when they held the championship of Jones County. He was the laziest ball player I ever set my peepers on, and yet no one can deny that he was the father of the automoroller skates.

"As a pitcher the Dean had no equal; ten strike-outs in one game on thirty balls pitched was considered nothing for him. And yet we knew right well that the only reason he took such pains to fan a batter out was that it only took three balls to do the trick, while if he should ever let a man walk to first it would require at least four efforts, and there'd be one more batter to dispose of. When it came to fielding he was all right there. Flies, liners, bounders— he froze on to 'em all. Why? Just because he knew that if he ever dropped the ball he'd have to stoop to pick it up. Pure laziness. Why, would you believe it, he wouldn't even take the trouble to sit down on the players' bench between innings. 'What's the use?' he'd say. 'You only have to get up again when the other side comes to bat.'

"The only thing that made us really peevish with the Dean, however, was his conduct at the bat. Rather than have to run to first he'd invariably strike wild at every ball, whether it came high, low, wide or over. Well, sir, you can imagine how he felt when one day the opposing pitcher hit him with the ball and forced him to amble down to first. That seemed bad enough to the Dean, but when Bull Thompson, the next man up, lined out a homer his anger knew no bounds. The Bull had to grab him by the shirt collar and trousers and push him all the way around the bases. By the time they'd crossed the plate the Dean broke loose and made a rush at Bull.

" 'That's a nice trick,' he roared. 'Oh, no; I suppose you didn't knock that home run on purpose, did you! If I pitch too swift when you're trying to catch, why don't you come out and say so like a man instead of trying to even up your low-down, sneaking, underhand tricks!'

"That put us in a pretty fix—our pitcher so dead sore on the catcher that they wouldn't speak, and the annual game with the Ringtail Roarers only ten days off. Soon after we reached home, however, Dean began to feel ashamed of his baby conduct and made it all up. For the next few days he kept pretty much to himself, but that didn't worry us, for he always took long sleeps when preparing for a great effort.

"The day of the big game came at last, and such a sight as the grounds were I never expect to see again. It seemed as if every man, woman and child in Jones County had come to town for the occasion. The Sheriff had previously torn down the fences in order to satisfy the demands of a dealer who had a chewing-gum account against the management, and the crowds were spread out on the grass for a quarter of a mile.

"When the Dean came to bat in the second inning the Roarers were one run to the good and we all felt some anxiety as to how he would act.

" 'Buck up and hit the ball, old man,' pleaded Captain Slugger Burrows.

"The Dean simply smiled and began to undo a paper box which he had kept tucked under his arm. He took out what at first appeared to be a pair of ordinary roller skates. As he adjusted them to his feet, however, we noticed that they had a complicated series of stops and levers running up the sides with a steam whistle and bell attachment. He paid no attention to the astonishment of the crowd, but glided gracefully up to the plate. The first ball pitched he basted far out into left. For a moment or two he stood motionless. Then there was a sharp wheezing of steam and he suddenly shot forward toward first. At first base a simple turn of a lever switched him off in the direction of second. The Roarers' short stop stood dumfounded in the middle of the base line. Clang! clang! clang! went the gong and the Dean sped on. By the time he had rounded third base the people had partially recovered from their surprise and the reception they gave the Dean was deafening. Men were dancing on each other's toes and embracing other men's wives. And above the mighty shouts of joy could be heard the sweet strains of 'When Johnnie Comes Marching Home' as distributed by the Lightfoot Lily Band. Dean's only comment, as he rolled up to the players' bench at half speed, was: 'I must get a fender, it's dangerous as it is.'

"Well, sir, thrice more did the Dean tie the score, and thrice more did the crowd go wild with glee. When he came to bat in the eleventh inning with the score 17—17, Captain Burrows could no longer control his curiosity.

" 'For Heaven's sake, what are they, Dean? How do they work?'

" 'They're automoroller skates,' replied the Dean. 'I'll explain when I get home.'

"But he never did, poor chap. He hit the ball all right, and he started for first all right. But when he went to turn for second the steering lever snapped, and he couldn't change his course. On he went out into right field.

" 'Help, help! Stop me! he cried with a heart-rending look of terror. But the people seemed in a trance and mechanically sank back to make way for him. On he sped. Once he was lost to sight in some valley only to rise again on the crest of a hill beyond. Soon he became only as a fly speck against the sinking sun. Then, after a farewell flicker or two he was absorbed entirely by the glaring ball of fire in the far West. The game was never finished.

"Where he is now I don't know. Several years later I heard he had a job as Rip Van Winkle in a wax-works tableau up State. The management fired him, though, because he snored. Poor old Dean!"

IV.

THE FAT EX-MASCOT OVERTRAINS.

"**W**ell, why is it you never played baseball yourself?" asked a latter-day fan of the very stout man sitting in the corner. 'You say you were the mascot for the famous Lightfoot Lilies of Jones County, and yet, with the exception of the time that they put you in to force the winning run in the thirteenth by being hit in the stomach, you never seem to have played yourself. After such successful daring were you never asked to play again? I don't quite understand."

The stout man gazed at the speaker searchingly for a few minutes, and then, apparently satisfied that the questions were asked in good faith, proceeded to unfold the one dark shadow in his otherwise sunny life.

"Have you never heard?" he began. "Then now you shall hear, and though I think no blame should rest with me, you yourself shall judge of that. Listen. You have already referred to the contest in which I forced the winning run owing to the pitcher's inability to put the ball over the plate without striking my corporation. This, I believe, was due to a law of physics which states that but one body can occupy the same space at the same time or words to that effect. But whatever the cause, I acquired a reputation for highclass baseball second to none in Jones County, and at once got a regular position on the team. My figure being my stock in trade, Captain Slugger Burrows of the Lightfoots spared no pains in bringing me to physical perfection before the next game with the Roarers. Under a carefully selected diet of beer, butter, lard, potatoes and cod liver oil I rapidly rose from a meagre 320 pounds to the magnificent figure of 412.

"For the first eight innings of the great contest which ultimately proved my downfall, I fully sustained my enviable reputation for artistic ball playing. Three times the bases were full with the Roarers

one run in the van. Three times I proved the Lightfoots' salvation by forcing the tying run by means
of my superior figure. Three times the home rooters vied with one another in futile attempts to pay
me suitable homage. I was truly more than queen.
And then that fatal ninth with its brimful cup of
gumless bitters! Four hundred and twelve pounds
of shattered idol!

"In the last half of the ninth I reached first through
my customary strategy. Later I succeeded in gain-
ing third by a daring bit of base running while the
Roarers' fielders were searching for Bull Thompson's
liner on the other side of the centre field fence.
Sammie Salmon and one of the Foote twins died
easy deaths on infield pop-flies. There we were:
Ringtail Roarers, 17; Lightfoot Lilies, 16; two out.
Thompson and yours truly on second and third
bases respectively, and the invincible Home Run
Hankins at the bat. All were breathless with suspense. The pitcher swung his arm back slowly and
then, swish, bang! Home Run Hankins never missed
his aim. I struggled bravely toward the plate, and
in less time than it takes to tell it Thompson was at

my back pushing violently. I doubled my efforts. A moment later Hankins himself caught up and joined in the single-file struggle for home and victory. 'Twas do or die, and the people were like lunatics in their wild excitement. Spurred on by their cheers I was soon but five feet from the plate, with Thompson and Hankins still dancing at my heels. Then suddenly a voice rose clearly above the others. 'Slide, Willie, slide!' it rang out. Oh, fatal words!"

At this moment the fat ex-mascot was overcome by emotion and stopped short. It was some minutes before he could pull himself together sufficiently to go on with his sad story.

"Well," he said at last, "I slid. Diving gracefully forward, I slid a nicely calculated slide that brought my chest directly above the rubber. But the enthusiasm this occasioned among the Lilies was short-lived.

" 'Touch the plate, you fool, touch the plate,' Bull Thompson and Hankins yelled together.

"Now, would you believe it, sir, try as I would I couldn't. My corporation had been overtrained.

Lying face down I was so high from the ground that my arms would not reach the plate.

" 'Rock me,' I cried, 'Rock me!'

" 'Rock you?' Bull Thompson roared. 'Rock you? We'll rock you, stone you, egg you, and— touch that plate, d'ye hear?'

" 'Rock me,' I pleaded with tears in my eyes. 'You don't understand. Rock me like you would a rocking horse. Tilt me. I can't touch bottom.'

" 'Twas too late. While I had been explaining my predicament to those blockheads the Roarers' fielders found the ball, and—er—well, we lost. Afterward I told Captain Slugger Burrows how it happened and begged for just one more chance. No use. He said that any fool with my shape ought to have sense enough to slide on his back, and that—but say, honest Injun, now, do you think I was in any way to blame?"

JIM TIMPSON *who got* RELIGION.

V.

JIM TIMPSON GETS RELIGION.

"Yes," said the ex-mascot of the Lightfoot Lilies, "taking everything into consideration, I suppose that Old Dean Braley was the finest pitcher that ever twirled the sphere in Jones County. But the man we signed after he left us pitched ball for a while that would have made the Dean's work look like a beer cork in a champagne bottle. Why, if Jim Timpson, that was the youngster's name, hadn't gone and got religion he'd be at the top of the big League today.

"It was rather peculiar the way we ran across him. While Captain Slugger Burrows and Sammie Salmon were taking a long walk one Sunday they noticed a boy standing out in front of a barn with his back to the door. He wore a big baseball mitt and was catching apples, one after another. Slugger said afterward that it was the most uncanny sight he ever laid his lookers on. There didn't seem to be any one throwing the apples and you couldn't see where they were coming from. But on they came—thump, thump, thump—plump in the middle of the mitt every clip. It was fully five minutes before they finally came to a stop. When the kid with the mitt saw the look of amazement on the faces of Slugger and Sammie he grinned from ear to ear.

" 'It's brother Jim,' he explained. 'He's 'round th' side th' barn practisin' outs. He'll shift to t'other side purty soon, I reckon, and practise ins.'

"Sure enough, as he spoke apples began to come thumping into the mitt again with almost incredible speed, and by watching closely they could see that they all came shooting around from the right side of the barn. Slugger and Sammie rushed a-round the corner. There stood a long, lean, red-headed gazabo with a pile of apples in one arm, socking 'em around the barn for dear life with the other. When he saw Slugger and Sammie he stopped.

" 'Wal,' he drawled.

" 'Say, young feller,' Slugger said, breathlessly, 'do you know you're wastin' yer opportunities here? Do you know you're about the finest durn curve distributor that ever—say, Rube, will you sign with the Lightfoot Lilies? You come round to Lily Park for practice tomorrow and we'll make it worth your while.'

" 'I'll speak to pa about it,' the hayseed said with an air of indifference, and picking out a fresh apple he started socking 'em 'round the corner again.

"Well, sir, Jim Timpson showed up for practice next day, and he more than made good right from the start. Outs, ins and drops, he couldn't be beat. And he was an ambitious cuss, too. Why, one day Bull Thompson found him standing on his head, waving his arms like a Baxter street clothier.

" 'What on earth are you up to now?' the Bull asked.

" 'Why, it's just like this,' answered Jim, springing onto his feet with a double back flipflop. 'You see there's only one curve I can't pitch and that's a slow up-shoot. Now, we play the Ringtail Roarers next Saturday, and I thought if I could only learn to pitch a drop standing on my head, it might serve the purpose just as well.' Did you ever hear the equal of that for earnest ball playing?

"Jim's downfall took place the day before the big game. His father sent him word that there was to be a shouting Methodist camp-meeting three miles north of the farm, and told Jim to be sure and come. Slugger gave him permission, and I will say for the Cap that that was the only mistake I ever knew him to make. When Timpson ambled back into town next day he had a meek, worn expression about the eye, and looked like a before-taking advertisement generally. Slugger thought it was lack of sleep, but old Doc Quackenbush said the boy had religion, and I guess the Doc was right. All through the game that day he pitched in a half-hearted, don't-care-if-I-do fashion, and when we came to the bat in the last half of the ninth with the score 12—11 in the Roarer's favor, we considered ourselves lucky that it wasn't worse.

"Slugger Burrows opened up with a two-bagger, the Foote twins died at first, Salmon connected for a single and Bull Thompson drew a base on balls. There we were; two out, three on bases and Jim Timpson, a left-handed hitter, at the bat. We only needed one run to tie the score and the crowd was rooting like a bunch of silver poplars. Well, sir, you can imagine the excitement when the very first ball pitched caught Jim square in the jaw. Our gang yelled as if all Bedlam was on a chowder party. But suddenly they stopped short in their rejoicing. Why didn't Timpson start for first and force in the winning run?

" 'No,' said Jim, pointing his hand impressively at the Roarers' pitcher. 'No, mine enemy hath struck me on the right cheek; I will turn my left.'

"Slugger Burrows argued with him, pleaded with him, threatened him and cursed at him. But all to no purpose. That pesky hayseed wouldn't have it any other way but that he should shift round and bat right-handed.

"Did he get what was coming to him on the other cheek? Not on your tintype. The backsliding infidel, who did the pitching for the Roarers put the next three across the plate for the prettiest strike-out you ever saw. After that it was all up with Jim

Timpson. I tried to put in a good word for the boy, but Slugger Burrows wasn't listening.

" 'Back to the barn with him,' he cried. 'My conscience won't stand for Sunday baseball, even on week days.' "

VI.

STUMP GREENWOOD'S WOODEN ARM.

"I see by the newspapers," mused the ex-mascot of the Lightfoot Lilies, "that a professional baseball catcher ran into a grandstand while trying to capture a foul the other day and broke his arm. They speak as if he wouldn't be able to get in the game again for some time, but I don't see why that should necessarily follow. One of the best all-around players I ever saw had a wooden arm, and instead of being a hindrance, that game wing of his gave him an advantage over every other man on the team.

"His name was Stump Greenwood, and his right arm was cut off close to the shoulder. They say he lost it trying to pinch the bait out of a neighbor's fox trap.

"The first we ever saw of him was when he trotted out to third base in the annual game with the Ringtail Roarers. We naturally felt a little sore at first to think that an old standby like Nip Tucker should be displaced by a new guy with a wooden arm, but, say, as the game went on his playing was a revelation. He froze on to everything he could reach with his good hook, and when the ball came the other side of him he'd swing that old peg of his and swat it over to the man nearest him. Once he got a fly on his sick side and banged it over to first for a double play before the runner could get back. That kind of jarred the scorer for a moment, but he finally fixed matters up by giving Stump two assists, one for throwing the ball over in time to catch the runner, and one for enabling the first baseman to catch the fly before it touched the ground. The first baseman was credited with two put-outs, doubly assisted, on the same play. That score book looked like a Chinese laundry ticket before the game was over.

"Stump only missed aim once. That was in the first of the fifth, when he tried to paste a liner over to first for a double. He swung his peg a little too soon and the ball caught the base runner square in the neck. The runner didn't mind getting hit so much, but when the umpire declared him out for interfering with a batted ball, he thought that that was rubbing things in a little too hard. But that wasn't what broke the game up. The real trouble began in the seventh when Stump was at the bat. The first ball pitched was a wild inshoot. He tried his best to dodge, but the ball hit his arm and rolled down the third base line for the prettiest little bunt you ever saw. By the time the Roarers had recovered from their surprise Stump was standing safe on second. They immediately set up a howl that he hadn't hit the ball, but that the ball had hit his arm and that therefore he was only entitled to one base on a dead ball. They were so persistent in their kicking that we finally conceded the point, and Stump was called back to first. Things rested quietly after that until the ninth.

"It was in the last half of the inning. The score was tied, two were out, the bases full, and Stump was at the bat. The very first crack out of the box he lined the ball toward second for what looked

like a two-bagger, but Cy Priest, the Roarers' pitcher, shot up in the air and made a miraculous catch
with his left. The Roarers started in from the field
thinking the side was out and the mob began to
root for an extra inning.

" 'Hold on!' yelled the umpire. 'Dead ball; the
Lightfoots win. It was decided before that that
hickory limb of his is an arm and not a bat. We must
be consistent.'

"Well, sir, you can imagine the rumpus that
caused. The spectators crowded onto the field and
the contest broke up in a rough house discussion
as to whether Stump's arm was a bat or his bat an
arm.

"Kind fate alone intervened to preserve harmony
between the baseball magnates of Jones County,
and make future contests possible. Stump Greenwood never played again. Going home from the
game that night we ran into a thunderstorm and
every one of us got wet to the skin. Next day Stump
tried to dry his arm out over an oil stove in time for
afternoon practice and the pesky thing warped.
We sandpapered it and put it in splints but all to

no purpose. Stump had lost his batting eye forever. He was never able to get another arm just the right weight or balance, and he had to give up athletics entirely. Instead of athletics, perhaps I should say baseball, for although I don't talk golf myself, I have a friend who does, and he tells me that there's a wooden armed man named Stump Greenwood out in southern Arizona whose marvelous lofting game is only surpassed by his wonderful putting."

VII.

A CROSS-EYED UMPIRE ASSERTS HIMSELF.

"Well, sir, I went to a professional baseball game the other day." The fat ex-mascot of the Lightfoot Lilies said this is a far-away tone that gave his friends the impression that he had not thoroughly enjoyed himself.

"And you didn't like it?" suggested one of them.

"Oh, yes," the fat ex-mascot replied hastily. "It was an exciting game, all right; it was one of the closest contests I've ever seen. Why, they had to play four extra rounds, and at that it ended in a draw. The referee—the umpire, I mean—called the contest on account of a foul. Some one threw the catcher's mask at him and it struck below the belt. Oh, yes, it was a good game all right. Somehow, though, it seemed different from the old Jones

County games. In those days we never even thought of questioning the fairness of the umpire's decisions. Hold on though,—yes, there was just one time that I'd almost forgotten about.

"It was one of the big championship contests between the Ringtail Roarers and the Lightfoot Lilies. Old Doc Quackenbush had been slated to do the officiating, but at the last moment he received a hurried call from out in the country—twins or scarlet fever, I don't remember—and there we were without an umpire. And in those days, you know, the umpire was considered a necessary evil to every ball game. So after a long discussion Captain Slugger Burrows of the Lilies and Captain Cy Priest of the Roarers agreed to pick some one from the crowd that could fill the place.

"They were walking up and down in front of the bleachers looking the gang over when the Slugger's face suddenly lit up.

" 'Hey,' he said, grasping Cy by the arm. 'Do you see that little cross-eyed gazabo up in the top row? Well, I choose him.'

" 'His peepers look as if they had been crossed

in love, but if he suits you, why I'm game. Hello, you with the tangled lamps!' Cy shouted; 'will you umpire?'

" 'Sure,' replied the little fellow eagerly, and he scrambled down on to the field.

"Slugger Burrows won the toss and chose outs. The little cross-eyed umpire picked out a mask and took his place behind the catcher—Bull Thompson always caught off the bat, whether there were men on base or not. The first man up for the Roarers knocked a low one to third and Foote scooped it in without leaving the bag. It looked a little like a pick-up, to be sure, but the umpire said 'Out,' and no one had the face to kick. The next man singled to left.

" 'Out for running out of base line,' piped up the umpire.

" 'What!' Cy Priest roared. 'Why that man ran as straight as a die. Do you—'

" 'Out,' repeated the little umpire, with a wave of his hand, and that settled it. Cy slunk back to the bench and picked out a bat. "As he stepped up to the plate I noticed a cunning twinkle in his eye,

STUMP GREENWOOD, THE ONE-ARMED MAN

but thought nothing of it at the time. He tapped the first ball pitched for an easy little grounder down toward short. The Slugger gobbled it in and shot it over to first for an easy out. The crowd was just getting ready to let loose when to their amazement Cy started down the third base line like a scared Filipino.

" 'Safe,' the umpire said, as Cy made third without any opposition.

" 'Safe?' bellowed Bull Thompson, throwing his mask on the ground and turning on the umpire fiercely. 'Safe? Why, you gol durned sawed-off little shrimp, where do you think first base is, anyway? I've half a mind to—'

"But he didn't. The umpire made one rush at him, and catching him round the legs stood him on his head as neatly as you please. That little runt shook the Bull until he was red in the face and then setting him down proceeded to gather up the change that had fallen out of his pockets.

" 'Five, ten, twenty-five,' he counted. 'Twenty-five, fifty, fifty-one, two, three—fifty-three. Is that all the money you've got? Well, then, you're fined fifty-three cents for abusive language. Now get off the grounds. Hustle!' And the Bull scrambled to his feet without a murmur and hustled.

"Now when Slugger Burrows picked out that umpire he thought was a wily fox, never dreaming that Cy Priest would get wily too. You see the little fellow was so cross-eyed that when he stood behind the bat, instead of seeing first with his right peeper, he saw it with his left, which should have been aimed down toward third. And his left looker, instead of having third base straight ahead, was crossed over on to first. Consequently he saw the whole diamond exactly reversed, and that's what caused his queer decisions.

"Did we put in a new umpire? Never even thought of it. We simply ran the bases the wrong way round for the rest of the game. It was just as fair for one side as for the other, and we didn't want to hurt the umpire's feelings."

VIII

PINK PERKINS AND HIS SCURVY METHODS

"**Y**ou may talk about the sweeping curves and parabolic shoots of the present-day baseball pitchers," said the fat man who was at one time mascot for the Lightfoot Lilies of Jones County, "but there isn't one of 'em that could have held a candle to old Pink Perkins the last season he did the twirling for the famous Ringtail Roarers. He'd probably be in the business now if the Lightfoot Lilies hadn't exposed his tricky methods in their annual game with the Roarers that summer. The funny part of it was that the season before he couldn't pitch anything but a straight ball and even the high school teams used to touch him up for a dozen hits or so every game. As for us we smothered him.

"But the very next season he blossomed out with

those wonderful curves. Why, a visitor to town said that in one game he saw Perkins pitch an out-curve so close to the plate that the batter struck at it. The ball kept right on curving until it came a-round to first base and caught the runner napping. The next ball pitched was an inshoot which not only drew another strike out of the batter, but which curved around to third base and caught a runner there. The catcher, according to the visitor's story, wasn't really needed, but played in the field just to fill out the batting list.

"Well, of course we put all such talk as this down as hot-air fund contributions, but we knew that there must be some foundation in the reports that Perkins was pitching very slick baseball. And right we were. When the big game came along he put it all over us and for eight innings not one of us touch-ed first except the first baseman when he was in the field. Bull Thompson, Home Run Hankins, and even Captain Slugger Burrows himself were all at Perkins' mercy. They struck at outs they couldn't reach; they let ins go by that shot over the plate, in fact, they did everything but connect with the ball. Then came the fatal exposure in the ninth. Little Sammie Salmon, the first man up for us, fell flat on his face to dodge the first ball pitched, but it curved straight over the rubber for a strike. The next one was one of Perkins' slow 'change' balls, and Sammie held out his bat to bunt. Thud! You can imagine his surprise when he started for first to find the ball stuck fast to the end of his bat. Pink Perkins made a rush for him, but the boys held him back and the secret was out. The Roarers' pitcher had been sticking chewing gum on the ball and the extra twist obtainable made his wonderful curves possible. The umpire, of course, forfeited the game to the Lilies, 9—0. But that wasn't the end. The Roarers had discovered that Captain Slugger Burrows wore a fly-paper mitt at shortstop, and although the most ignorant child knows that fly-paper is made for catching flies, the umpire gave the game to them also, making the score a tie at 9—9. What followed is best left untold. As the *Jones County Courier* said, it was a 'game of forfeits with the kissing left out.' "

IX.

PROF. MEETEER AND HIS WONDERFUL LENS.

"Straight old-fashioned baseball always wins out in the long run," the fat ex-mascot of the Lightfoot Lilies once declared to some friends. "Tricks are never reliable, and they're sometimes even dangerous. Why just look at the wily stunt the Lilies put up on the Ringtail Roarers in the final game in '89. And what did it all amount to? Two men knocked unconscious and the contest broken up in a rough-house. That's the kind of a trick the Lilies played. It would never have happened if 'The Ring Brothers' Stupendous Circus and Educational Side Show' hadn't struck town three days before the big game. It would never have happened if the whole Lily team hadn't attended said stupendous circus with its aforementioned educational side show. But tears of remorse won't solder a leaking growler. To my story!

"As I said, we did the circus and side show, and did 'em brown. Bull Thompson fed the elephants, little Sammie Salmon was completely won by Daisy, the fat lady, and old Dean Braley had the time of his life practising in-shoots on a nigger's head stuck through a sheet. Before we could drag him away he had touched up the artful dodger for forty-seven alleged cigars. We filed out of the tent thinking we'd seen the whole show, when we ran into a guy with a big telescope. According to his shingle he was Prof. Meeteer, the world-famed astronomer, who not only managed all the stars, but who had inside information on the secret workings of the moon as well.

" 'Step up, gents!' he was yelling. 'Till you've seen this you've seen nothing. The atmospheric conditions could not be more favorable for scientific research. Ha! What's that? As sure as I live the Dog Star has the Great Bear on the run. And the Little Dipper's leaking; that's what makes the Milky Way. Gents, you run absolutely no risk; I stake my reputation upon my words. And there's Venus! Think of it, gents; Venus revealed at 10 cents per! And—'

" 'Venus for mine,' growled Bull Thompson, diving into his pocket for the necessary dime.

"After the Bull had squinted through the pesky machine for a few minutes his ardor for Venus cooled somewhat, and he made way for the rest of the bunch who were thirsting after knowledge. While all this was going on Captain Slugger Burrows had kept in the background. Suddenly he slapped his leg joyfully and rushed up to the Professor.

" 'My learned friend,' he said taking the astronomer by the arm, 'will'st stroll with me a while, forsooth? I wouldst a few words with thee concerning the magnitude and possibilities of your noble science.'

"The Professor saw there was something doing. ' 'Tis well,' he said, and arm in arm they walked up and down in front of the tent. It was evident from the Slugger's gestures that he was throwing one awful game of 'con' into the Professor, but what it was we couldn't tell. We only caught snatches of the talk as they were passing. 'Can it be done?', the Slugger asked on one of these occasions. 'Well,' we heard the Professor reply, 'weather conditions being favorable, it is within the possibilities of sci—.' Finally, their conference came to an end; and they returned to the telescope, where the Foote twins were engaged in a heated argument as to which of the Gemini was which.

" 'Saturday at three,' the Slugger said as we were about to leave. 'And, oh, Professor, I forgot to ask your terms.'

" 'Twenty-five plunkets spot, and,' he said thoughtfully, 'a guarantee of decent burial in case of detec—'

" 'S-s-s-!' whispered the Slugger, and he led us away. Going home he said nothing about the nature of his conversation with the Professor, and none of us thought to ask him. In fact, by the time we reached our downy beds sweet memories of that fair fat lady, the beautiful Circassian girl, the sinuous snake charmer and the sad-eyed two-headed singer had driven all else from our minds.

"The sun shone merrily Saturday afternoon and

Lily Park was packed to the limit. All the fence space, knotholes and telegraph poles had been sold out the week before, and a guy from the State Fair was coining money hand over fist selling choice seats in a captive balloon that he had anchored to the roof of the grandstand. At three o'clock the balloon ascended and the game began. In the first inning neither side scored. The Roarers crossed the rubber twice in the second, but the Lilies, thanks to a base on balls and Bull Thompson's home run, managed to even matters up in their half. It was in the third inning that strange things came to pass. Slats McManus, the first man up for the Roarers, drew his base on four wide ones. Then Cy Priest ambled to the plate. We noticed that as he toed the rubber he began to sniff and hold his nose at a proud angle, but thought nothing of it at the time. The first ball went wild.

" 'Whew!' said Cy. 'Was that a dead ball, Mr. Umpire?"

"The umpire ignored him. Cy planted his feet firmly and with a vicious swing caught the next one square on the nose for a through trip over the right field fence. Slats McManus darted for second like a fleeting thought, and the Roarer gang went hoarse with joy. But their glee stopped with a sudden jar. What was the trouble with Cy? Why didn't he run? Then they saw it all—the home plate was melting and that was what had caused Cy's contemptuous sniffing. In starting for first he had certainly put his foot in it in every sense of the word. In vain he tried to free himself from the sticky rubber. Finally, in desperation he got down on his hands and knees and began to crawl toward first base with the rubber still sticking to his shoe. Slats was just rounding second. Cy, encouraged by the shouts of the visiting rooters, was now almost half way to the bag. But the tension on the rubber grew greater as the distance increased, and it was only by the fiercest kind of digging that he was now able to make headway. Slats passed third and was coming down the home stretch. Cy, by herculean efforts, had managed to get within ten feet of first. Our fielder was still chasing the ball. On Cy crawled. But would the home plate stand the strain? That was the question. Now he was clawing the ground only two feet from the bag, when—Bang! He was shot back as from a catapult and landed against Slats McManus's chest, five yards the other side of where home was before it left. Cy's weight had been unequal to the tension. Wouldn't that rattle the shingles off the roof of your mouth?

"Cy and Slats lay motionless on the ground where they had collided. The players quickly gathered around them, and the crowds swarmed over the railings onto the field. They almost smothered the two men with whiskey, smelling salts, brandy and wet towels, but all to no purpose. Suddenly the people were attracted by the antics of a little guy on the outskirts of the bunch. He was dancing around like an angry grasshopper and pointing wildly above his head. All glanced upward. They were struck dumb with amazement. There in the captive balloon above them was none other than my old, world famed, circus friend, Prof. Meeteer. He was leaning over the side of the balloon basket, smiling benignly on the upturned faces below. In his hand he held the front window of his telescope, still focused on the spot where home plate formerly rested. The crowd was on in a minute. He had been using that telescope window as a sun glass to melt the rubber. For a moment there was an ominous silence. Then a rumbling, roaring howl of rage, and in less time than it takes to tell it the whole grandstand roof was one seething mass of snarling Ringtail rooters.

"The Professor's benign smile immediately gave way to a look of abject terror. One man was already half way up the cable holding the balloon. The Professor withdrew from sight, only to reappear a moment later clutching a long carving knife in his right hand. The crowd paused in their mad scramble to see what his next move would be. That pause was the Professor's salvation. Ducking over the side, he made a quick pass with his knife, and, swish! The man climbing the rope tumbled back onto the roof, and at the same instant the balloon shot skyward at the rate of about ninety miles a minute. Up, up, up it went. The crowd looked on with open mouths and staring eyes until there was nothing left to look on. The game was never finished.

"No, the Professor never returned to collect his twenty-five bones, and I'm not so sure he wasn't wise at that. For a time, at any rate, it looked more like the decent burial proposition for his."

X.

WILL SEYMORE BALKS AT BLINDERS.

"No, I haven't played baseball this summer," the fat man told his friends. "My interest in the national game is as great as ever; my arm has none of its old-time cunning; my feet are as nimble as of yore, but my eyesight is rapidly going back on me. Not but what I've known ball players with eye troubles—but they've labored under difficulties which I should never care to face. For example? Well, let me see. There was big Will Seymore, our old second baseman. Taking everything into consideration he was about the best player with bum blinkers that I ever knew. He wasn't near-sighted or far-sighted, nor was he cross-eyed. But his peepers were both so gol-darned ugly-looking that each instinctively turned away from the other as far as possible. Squint-eyed, wall-eyed, or something like that. Just opposite from the cross-eyed, y'know.

"Why, it was so bad that whenever Will Seymore crossed a crowded street he was able to watch for trolleys in both directions without so much as turning a hair. And once while marching in a political parade with his head straight to the front he dumbfounded the captain with the information that the men on each end of the line were out of step. I really do believe that if that man had ever tried to take a philosophical view of the present, he'd have got views of both the dim past and the distant future instead.

"The first time Slugger Burrows ever saw Seymore was in New York the year of the Brotherhood League. If you remember the Brotherhood grounds were on the block above those of the National League. Seymore was standing on the roof of a hansom in the street between them watching both games at the same time. I don't know how the Slugger ever got next to his ability as a ball tosser, but he did all right, for ten days later Seymore was out in Jones County holding down second base for us in the practice games preparatory to the big championship match with the Ringtail Roarers.

"And say, maybe His Eyelets wasn't the real thing, though! He would stand there on second facing the plate, with one looker fastened on third and the other staring the runner at first square in the face. It would have taken better than a second-story man to have stolen a base on that guy. But it was his stick work that attracted most attention in the game with the Ringtail Roarers. Three singles, one homer, and three bases on balls out of seven times at bat. He seemed to know just when the ball was coming over, and tricky curves and shoots that would have fooled even the Slugger himself had no terrors for big Will Seymore. Still that wasn't so remarkable when all the circumstances of the case are taken into consideration. You see when he was at the bat, while one eye was gazing intently at the pitcher, the other one was carefully scanning the catcher. In that way he was able to read the latter's signals and in consequence knew just what kind of a ball to expect from the former.

"What were his troubles then? I'm coming to

that. Throughout the first eight innings of the big game his fielding was above reproach, and the Ringtail Roarers were looking like new business for the undertaker. Then the unforeseen happened. Cy Priest, the first man up for the Roarers, drew his base on balls. Will had him covered with his left optic and that, of course, focused his other looker over onto third. On the next ball pitched Cy made a dash for second. Our catcher shot the ball down to nip him off, and—thud! Four teeth and a brokken nose; that's all. Don't you see it. Seymore didn't either. Since he had one eye levelled on first and the other on third, the ball, thrown from home, came right in between his two lines of vision, just where he couldn't see it.

"Now Seymore was too good a player to release for a little misfortune like that. When he recovered from his injuries sufficiently to show up for practice again we tried having the catcher throw either to first or third, where the baseman would pass the ball along to second. But this method was too slow. Every man, woman and child who had the best interests of the Lightfoot Lilies at heart set to thinking to discover some way in which it would be possible to keep Seymore at second. It was old Doc Quackenbush, the town physician and oculist, who finally solved the problem. He rigged up a pair of horse blinders lined with looking glasses. These mirrors were arranged at such angles to enable Seymore to see all objects directly in front of him.

"Well, His Eyelets was tickled all over when the scheme was first mentioned to him, even when he was told that he would probably have to wear the new paraphernalia night and day in order to get used to seeing like other people. He said no sacrifice could be too great to make for the national game.

"After he'd been in his new harness for a couple of days, however, he began to look at matters in a different light, figuratively as well as literally. He began to demur; then to fret and fume. Finally, eleven days after the introduction of the experiment, he balked completely. He rushed into Doc Quackenbush's office, tore the blinders from his face and slung them against the wall, shattering the mirrors into a thousand bits.

THE FOOTE TWINS, "RIGHT" AND "LEFT."

" 'Take your durned harness!" he yelled angrily. 'As for me, baseball be bust! Do you think I'm going to be bothered turning my head every time I want to look in a window?"

"Seymore took the first train out of town. The last I heard of him he was spotting shoplifters for a big Chicago department store."

XI.

WAS STEVE SPEED A FAST BASERUNNER?

"The fastest baserunner I ever saw," said the fat ex-mascot of the Lightfoot Lilies in comparing baseball of the season just past with that of the old days, "was little Sammie Salmon of the Lilies. But the fastest baserunner I ever heard of was, or wasn't, as the case may have been, Steve Speed, who played, or who didn't play, I don't know which, with the Ringtail Roarers. At any rate, whether there was a Steve Speed or not, and if there was, whether he played with the Roarers or not, he was certainly the fastest that ever came over the cross-ways. You don't understand? Well, I'll tell you all about him.

"One afternoon about a month before the last game we ever played with the Ringtail Roarers the boys were all sitting around in the Post Office discussing our chances for the big contest. Captain Slugger Burrows, who was tending Post Office that day, was over in the corner reading the ball news in a *Jones County Courier* that had accidentally slipped its wrapper before delivery. Suddenly he clutched the paper tightly and sprang to his feet.

" 'For heaven's sake, boys, listen to this: "We have it from a high source," he began to read breathlessly, "that the Roarers have unearthed a phenomenal baserunner, with whose services they feel confident of wresting the Jones County laurels from the erstwhile invincible Lightfoot Lilies. The newcomer's name is Steve Speed. His extraordinary ability was first discovered while he was in the box one day last week. He stopped an easy grounder and tossed it over to first to catch the runner. The ball had no sooner left his hands than, to his horror, he discovered that first was uncovered. Without a moment's hesitation he made a dive for the bag and succeeded in reaching it just in time to catch the ball that he had thrown but an instant before, thereby scoring a put-out and an assist unassisted."

" 'Boys,' said the Slugger, crumpling the paper savagely in his fists, 'to Lily Park with you. Practice begins at once. Hustle!' "

"Well, sir, that week we practised. In the morning the boys would all go down to the station and race the trains as they steamed out of town. Afternoons they'd ease up a bit and just indulge in short sprints paced by the trolley car. At night the daily practice would conclude with a brisk cross-country run around the township. The work began to show. At the end of the week we began to have some hopes of beating the Roarers after all. And then came a second copy of the *Courier,* knocking our hopes higher than taxes.

" 'The wonderful baseball feat performed by Steve Speed,' the article said, 'which was published exclusively by the *Jones County Courier,* has been eclipsed by an even more astonishing performance by the same player. We have it from the same high source from which we obtained our former news that Speed has now become so proficient in running that he is able to pitch the ball from the box and by an incredibly quick start reach the plate in time to catch the ball behind the bat. The Roarers have released their catcher.' Wouldn't that hasten your pulse? It did ours.

"And the next week's accounts were even worse. The *Courier* got it straight from their own private high source that this guy Speed was even better than the week before. He was now so super at the game that he not only ran down behind every plate and caught the balls that he himself had pitched, but in case the batter knocked a fly he darted out in the field and gobbled that too. The Roarers had, according to the *Courier,* released their whole outfield. When we read that, Bull Thompson wanted to cancel the game, but the Slugger wouldn't hear of it. 'The Lightfoot Lilies,' he said, 'may be made to look like Tarheel Thistles, but we won't wither before we're picked.'

"When the big game finally did come off the Roarers certainly had us on the run. For three innings they piled up runs almost at will. But then we began to get wise. Where was this fast-running phenom? Cy Priest was still in the pitcher's box and the whole outfield seemed to be in their usual places.

Perhaps he was sick. The thought gave us courage and we began to pick up a bit. You all know how we finally pulled the game out of the fire in the last half of the tenth. That's a matter of history now. Well after it was all over the Slugger went up to Cy Priest.

" 'Say,' he asked, 'where's that hot baserunner of yours, Cy?'

" 'You mean Steve Speed?' replied Cy with a funny look in his eye. 'Oh, we couldn't pay the salary he demanded and had to let him go. The last I heard of him he was touring the Northwest, playing exhibition games to enormous crowds.'

"Yes, sir, he was the best that ever was—if he was. As I said, I don't really know. Of course the *Courier* said they had it from a high source, but then—well, you know Cy Priest was over six feet."

XII

THE STAR ATTRACTION.

"**I**s there any penalty in this year's baseball rules for tampering with the grounds?" the fat ex-mascot asked. "No? Ah, well, wait until the game ascends to the lofty scientific plane it occupied in the good old Jones County days, when the Ringtail Roarers and the Lightfoot Lilies struggled to pluck the palm of victory from each other's brows. The rule framers will have a tight fit trying to keep abreast of the times when that happens.

"It was in '87 that the Roarers attempted to put through what was probably the most contemptible scheme ever hatched outside of a melodrama. Three consecutive seasons had the Goddess of Victory made our banner her perch. With the Roarers it was a case of do or die. They came near doing.

"There was a drizzling rain on the day of the big game that year, but rather than disappoint the enormous crowds that had gathered in Ringtail Grove, it was decided to pull the contest off in spite of the leaky weather. As we trotted out upon the diamond to inspiring strains from the band confidence expanded every Lily chest; victory was reflected in every Lightfoot eye.

"Sammie Salmon was the first man to bat for us. He lifted a little pop-fly over third which should have been good for a single. But just as he was within ten feet of the bag he stumbled and fell flat on his face. That was all right. Then came Bull Thompson. He rapped a slow one down toward second that seemed all to the good. But just as he reached the spot where Salmon had come to grief, he, too, took a tumble. Slugger Burrows, the third man up, was thrown out in the same way.

"Well, sir, that set us to shaking our thought-boxes some. Bull Thompson, it is true, interfered a bit when he first joined the team, but he got pretty well over that after we'd kept him on snow shoes for a couple of winters. While as for Sammie

Salmon and the Slugger, they were as fly on their pins as any guys that ever wore shoe cleats. We couldn't understand it. To make matters worse, after the Roarers had batted out seven runs in their turn with the stick, it was the same old story over again. Stump Greenwood, Sam Strong, Nip Tucker— they all took a spill in the same old spot, ten feet the home side of first. At the end of the fourth the score was 17 to good intentions, the Lilies having all the good intentions. We were considerably less inflated above the shoulders than when the game began.

"It was between the fourth and fifth innings that the explanation of it all came, and things that were things happened. That particular part of Mother Earth's bosom where the Lilies had been unwillingly coming to rest with such regularity had become so ruffled that the Slugger hauled out the hand-roller to level it off a bit. Cy Priest protested that the game was being delayed. Overrruled in this he asked that he be allowed to do the rolling. But the Slugger couldn't see it that way. He ran the old machine down the first base line until he reached the spot that needed smoothing. Kerchunk! That roller stopped with a jerk that almost created a vacuum in the Slugger. He got down on his hands and knees and began to examine the ground. Priest made a rush for him but the Lilies dragged him back. What do you suppose he unearthed there? What was probably the largest and most powerful magnet ever constructed, sir. It was so large and so powerful that every time a steel shoe-cleat came in contact with it the wearer was stopped short and thrown upon his face. 'Twas then that we noticed for the first time that the Roarers had worn their rubbers thoughout the game, and as rubbers, you know, are non-conductors, they were enabled to— What's that?: Well, you ask Slugger Burrows if you don't believe it."

XIII.

A JUMPING UMPIRE DEMORALIZES BOTH TEAMS.

"Say, you know that daffy dance that makes a guy jiggle up and down like a rubber ball in its last bounces, while his features twitch a ragtime accompaniment at right angles? The invitus dance, or something like that?" The fat ex-mascot of the Lightfoot Lilies looked inquiringly at his friends.

"Why, you mean the St. Vitus dance," one of them ventured.

"Is that it? Well, this St. Vitus may have been a good man and graceful dancer, but any time I want to trip the light fantastic just give me an old-fashioned waltz or something with a glide in it for mine. I once knew a baseball umpire that was proficient at his step. The Ringtail Roarers brought him down to the championship game at Lily Park one year when it was their turn to furnish the umpire. Say, you ought to have seen him as he stuttered out to take his place behind the bat. I'd be willing to back him odds-on against St. Vitus at his own dance and concede thirty twitches to the minute at that. But we could have stood for his dancing all right if he hadn't gummed the game the way he did. How? You couldn't guess in a rich uncle's lifetime. It was like this:

"Captain Priest of the Roarers won the toss and chose outs. For us Sammie Salmon dropped a neat little single back of third. Then the trouble began. Their third baseman tossed the ball over to first, and the first baseman clapped it onto Sammie, who by this time was anchored fast to the bag.

" 'How's that, Mr. Umpire?' shouted the first baseman.

" 'The umpire was still jumping up and down in the ecstacies of his saintly dance. 'You're—you're—outatfirst,' he spluttered, with a convulsive wave of his hand.

" 'What?' Sammie Salmon demanded, indig-

DEAN BRALEY AND HIS AUTOMOROLLER SKATES.

nantly. 'Out? Why, I've never left the base.'

"But in those days, you know, what the umpire said went, and there was nothing for Sammie to do but slink back to the bench and keep his troubles to himself. The same thing happened when Bull Thompson drew his base on balls. While he was standing on the bag the first baseman held the ball against his arm and again appealed to the umpire. Same result. Two men sitting on the bench with troubles of their own. Then came Captain Slugger Burrows. First on dead ball; stood on first with both feet; touched by first baseman; and side declared out by the saintly dance guy. That was more than we could stand. Slugger Burrows threatened to take his team off the field, and it was only by the strongest kind of argument that Cy Priest succeeded in persuading him to finish out the inning.

"Matters were finally adjusted and the Roarers took the bat. The first two men up died easy deaths on infield pop-flies. We began to have some hopes of a tie game in spite of the jiggling umpire. Then Cy Priest toed the rubber. He drove the first pill out of the box down between second and short, and reached first with a whole clock full of time to spare. Foote tossed the ball over to first just as a matter of form, when—'What's the trouble with Priest?' the rooters began to ask one another. 'Why, he's jumping too; is that spluttering umpire contagious?' All at once Captain Slugger Burrows at short burst out laughing. It seemed rather cruel to us to find merriment in the affliction of a rival. We didn't think it of the Slugger.

" 'Why, aren't you guys next?' he asked when the side was finally retired. 'You see the way that umpire jumps around? Well, that's a disease; he can't help it. What's more he doesn't even know it. Ha, ha, ha!' We were utterly disgusted with his heartless laughter. 'Don't you see it yet?' he asked when he had partly recovered. 'His umpirelets there watches the runner instead of the base. He thinks he's standing still and that it's the runner that's doing the jumping. He thinks we were all touched out while we were jumping in the air. The only way to make him think you're standing still is to jump up and down with him the way Cy Priest did. Don't you see it now?'

"Now what do you think of that? And the Slugger was right. We found that by jumping up and down with the St. Vitus umpire he thought we were literally on the level and consequently called us safe. Why, by the sixth inning the thing had become second nature, and the eighteen players of both teams were springing up and down like so many dyspeptic grasshoppers. Even the spectators seemed to catch the spirit of the thing. Men, women and children were jumping round in a way that at one time threatened destruction to the grandstands. 'Humph,' grunted the umpire when the thing was at its height, 'I knew—they'd get tired of their infernal jumping—and—and—have to quiet down—after awhile.' It would have made any other man dizzy to look at 'em.

"Who finally won the game? The Roarers; but they had to employ the scurviest kind of underhand methods to do it. It was in the first of the ninth. They were one run to the good, two men were gone, Bull Thompson was jumping hopefully on third and Home Run Hankins was at the bat. Suddenly some one on the Roarers' bleachers sang out, 'Hey, Bull Thompson! Your stocking's coming down.' The Bull started to stoop, and then, suspecting treachery quickly straightened up and resumed his jumping. Priest shot the ball over and the third baseman clapped it on the Bull.

" 'You're out at third!" the umpire shouted. 'Gee but you're jumping high!'

"The Bull's momentary hesitation had put him out of time with the umpire. They who hesitate are lost!"

XIV.

THE DUM-DUM DUMMIES SLIP UP AND FALL DOWN.

"That deaf and dumb baseball pitcher you're all talking about," the fat ex-mascot said, with an air of superior knowledge, "may make good for a time, but mark my words, gentlemen, in the long run he's going to slip up and fall down. I don't care how good he is now, no deaf, dumb or blind man can play gilt-edged baseball and keep it up. I've had experience and know what I'm talking about. When I was with the Lightfoot Lilies we ran up against about the hottest aggregation of that sort that ever cursed an umpire. It happened like this:

"You see the little disputes between the Ring-tail Roarers and the Lightfoot Lilies began to grow more and more serious, and finally the Jones County magnates decided that for the best interests of the game it would be necessary for the two teams to break off entirely. Then, of course, we had to scrape round to try to find some worthy rivals. We had just given the hunt up in despair, when one day Captain Slugger Burrows walked into the Post Office, smiling from ear to ear.

" 'Boys,' said he, 'I have here a letter from an old schoolmate of mine, blind, but general manager and second assistant janitor of the Jones County Eye, Ear and Tongue Infirmary. But to the point. He writes me that the patients of this worthy institution have formed a baseball team and feel the greatest confidence in their ability to put it all over the Lightfoot Lilies on the Lilies' own grounds next Saturday afternoon. Boys, is it a go?'

" 'Nothin' else,' they all shouted, and the postmaster closed up the office for afternoon practice.

"Well, sir, when Saturday afternoon came around Lily Park was jammed. Over in the bleachers where the Roarers' rooters used to sit were the Infirmary heelers, and I must say they were the queerest looking bunch I ever trimmed my lamps on. Deaf men, dumb men, blind men—there wasn't a real well guy

in the gang. As for the Dum-Dum Dummies themselves—that was the name the team traveled under—
for the first six innings they were revelations. Outside of the fact that some of the deaf ones couldn't
always tell whether they'd struck out or drawn a
base on balls, and except for the extra trouble the
umpire had in pushing them off the bases when they
were called out on close decisions, they played the
game for all there was in it. Yes, they were all good,
but the deaf guy at short, the dumb guy in the centre
and the guy with the stained glass eye on second
were the three particular stars that would turn
the Milky Way sour with envy.

"Why, it was the guy with the stained glass eye
who knocked the home run that put the Dum-
Dums ahead in the fourth. And, say, you ought
to have seen the reception he got when he crossed
the plate. Those that could see but were dumb
waved their arms; those that could speak but were
deaf passed the good word on to those that could
hear but were blind. In a minute the whole Infirmary people were yelling and screaming or waving
their arms with the exception of one little deaf,

dumb and blind girl who had come along just to get the fresh air.

"But do you remember what I told you in the beginning about these kind of players never lasting? Well, sir, it was these very three stars, the deaf guy, the dumb guy, and the guy with the stained glass eye who lost the game for the Dum-Dums in the last half of the seventh. The score was 5—3 in their favor, the bases were full, and Bull Thompson was at the bat for us. Bull popped up a little fly back of second that looked like sure death. The Light-foots groaned. But the Dum-Dum captain, just to avoid confusion, yelled 'Who's got it?' and that's what started all the trouble. The deaf guy couldn't hear him and started on the dead run for it from shortstop. The dumb guy in centre field tried to say in finger talk that he had it, but the guy with the bum lamp was on the wrong side and couldn't see what he said. The natural result was one grand collision during which everybody scored. The dumb guy recovered in plenty of time to throw Bull Thompson out at third, but his hands were so busy cursing the stained glass-eye man that he couldn't pick the ball up. At that our crowd simply went wild with joy, and they were possessed of all the faculties to do it with. The Lily Band struck up that heartrending ballad entitled 'They're More to Be Pitied Than Censured' in a way that drew tears from even the glass eyes of the visitors.

"That one mix-up seemed to take the heart right out of the Dum-Dum Dummies, for in the remaining two innings we crossed the plate almost at will The final score, if I remember rightly, was 33—7. Do you know I really felt sorry for that infirmary crowd as they filed out through the gates. 'Twas such a change from the bright and happy throng that had marched in but a few hours before. Then all were jubilant; now only two seemed to have one spark of gladness left—the little deaf, dumb and blind girl who had come for the air, and one poor, old, blind man. He said to a friend that it was the finest contest he had ever heard, and on account of his great age none had the heart to tell him of the true result. Poor old man!"

XV.

HARDIE FERMAIN'S IRON DUKES.

"Any guy who makes fun of a baseball player for wearing a big mitt or glove ought to throw a brick off a high roof and hang on to the brick. I have no use for him," said the fat ex-mascot. "The runner's out just as much when the ball comes to rest in the depths of a big bunch of athletic upholstery as when some smart Aleck freezes on to a hot one with one bare hook.

"Take the case of Hardie Fermain, who played second base for the Lilies against the Ringtail Roarers back in '83. He never would wear a glove. He said it was babyish. What was the consequence? Ah, well!"

The fat ex-mascot sighed.

"Hardie was a carpenter by trade. His hands were

naturally tough and he made them more so by catching liners barehanded.

"Not satisfied with this he got to walking round on his hands for an hour or two after practice every day. They finally became so callous that he could drive nails with his palms, and he gave up using a hammer in his trade.

"For the first four innings of the big championship game that year we made the Roarers look like a bunch of dead ones playing hookey from a cemetery. Three times had we crossed the plate, while as for them—goose eggs. This was chiefly due to a miraculous performance by Hardie Fermain at second.

"In the first half of the second the Roarers had the bases full, two were out and their heavy-hitting twirler, Cy Priest, was at the bat. The first ball pitched was a straight one. Crack!

"At almost the same instant Hardie Fermain shot three feet in the air. Thud! A moment later he was standing nonchalantly over second with the ball in his right hand.

"Well, sir, you never heard such pandemonium.

Irrespective of how their sympathies lay the 3,000 people present rose to their feet as though urged upward by 3,000 pins. Men howled and hugged each other; women went ladybug-house with joy.

"You will partially realize what a wonderful catch it was when I tell you that we afterward discovered two flat places on the ball; one where it had been struck by Cy's bat, and the other where it had come in contact with Hardie's hand. But to come to Fermain's downfall.

"It was in the Roarers' half of the fifth. Again the bases were full; again two were out, and once more the redoubtable Cy Priest faced the pitcher. Once more he hit the first ball pitched, but this time it was only a little pop-fly that soared into the iron dukes of Hardie Fermain.

"A wild cheer broke forth from the Lily fans. But horrors! The cheering stopped short and, as suddenly as it had arisen, gave place to a despairing groan. Hardie Fermain had dropped the ball.

" 'Pick it up! pick it up!' howled the Lilies as the Roarers started tearing around the bases.

"Hardie did pick it up. But before he drew back

his arm to throw he opened wide his hands and gazed with child-like wonder at the palms. The ball rolled to the ground.

"Four times he picked it up; four times he opened his hands, and four times the ball rolled back to the ground. It was not until the last Roarer had crossed the plate with what proved to be the winning run that he clutched the ball tightly with both hooks, and, with a convulsive effort, slung it toward the catcher.

"As you can readily imagine, this strange conduct drove the Lily crowd frantic with rage. They surged out on to the field, cursing and shaking their fists. It was only with the greatest difficulty that we succeeded in spiriting Hardie through the gate and down to the railroad in time to catch the first train out of town.

"Hardie was all broken up over the affair.

" 'My hands have got so hard,' he sobbed on the way to the station 'that I—can't feel—the easy ones any more. 'And—every time I opened—er— my hands—to see if I had it—er—the fool ball dropped—to the ground—again.'

"Now what do you think of that? Of course, just as soon as we found out what the trouble had been we patted him on the back and told him to cheer up. Little things like that, we said, were likely to happen to anyone.

"And before the train left we all shook hands with him to show him that things were all right. But he never knew it. His hands were so callous he couldn't feel it. He went away thinking we were still sore, when in reality the only hard feeling in the matter was on the part of Hardie's hands."

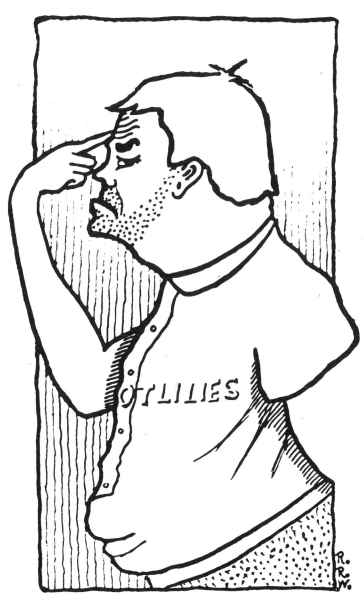

BULL THOMPSON WHO COULDN'T REMEMBER.

XVI.

TANGLEFOOT TOM PLAYS STRENUOUS BALL.

"Cowboys make pretty good baseball players," the fat ex-mascot of the Lightfoot Lilies admitted, rather doubtfully, "but they're hard to tame, very hard to tame. Now there was Tanglefoot Tom, good fielder, strong thrower, sure hitter, but—what? You've never heard of Tanglefoot Tom? Well, well, perhaps he was before your time.

"It was the day before one of our championship contests with the Ringtail Roarers. We were sitting around the post office table discussing our prospects for the morrow with faces the length of plumbers' bills. Captain Slugger Burrows had just broken it to us gently that Sammie Salmon was laid up in bed with ptomaine poisoning, thereby making us one man short in the outfield. Now, as you probably know, the Ringtail Roarers gave nine men all they could handle, while as for tackling them with only eight, it was as if Jonah had tried to swallow the whale.

"While we were at the most heartrending point of our sad conversation we were suddenly interrupted by a violent crash at the post office door. Biff! bang! and in clanked the wildest, wooliest looking gazabo you ever clapped your lookers on. Sombrero well down over his bushy brows, barbed wire mustachios, revolvered belt and spurs on his boots that would penetrate the most inward thoughts of the heartiest horse. He was cowboy for keeps, and, what's more, one of the kind that you'd want on your side when the rough-house starts.

" 'Well,' he growled after he had looked the boys over thoroughly, 'who's running this here joint? I want two bits wuth of yer best chewin'—fine cut preferred.'

"Captain Slugger Burrows—he had charge of the post office in those days—hastened behind the counter to weigh the tobacco.

" 'Say, strangers' said the latter after he had

stowed away one-half of his purchase in his cheek and the other half in his hip pocket, 'isn't thar any excitement doin' 'round these parts? The town seems like it's sorter waitin' fur the coroner.'

" 'Umph,' the Slugger grunted, indignantly, 'if you hang around here until tomorrow I guess you'll find there's life in this burg. Ringtail Roarers versus the Lightfoot Lilies at Lily Park for the baseball championship of Jones County. That's what's doing here, my young friend.'

" 'Baseball, pardner? Wal, that means that Tanglefoot Tom plants his stakes right whar he is. Why, d'ye know, pardner, that out in Dakota Territory I'm considered the durndest finest ball tosser that ever swung an umpire? Here I be and here I stay.'

"With that he drew up a box and slung his feet on the table like the rest of us.

" 'You play ball? asked the Slugger eagerly. 'Do you mean it? Put it here, my friend, put it here.'

"The captain at once began to explain our crippled condition, and said that if the newcomer would only consent to fill in the outfield he could have everything in the town that he wanted and take what he didn't want home to his friends.

" 'Will Tanglefoot Tom play in the outfield? Ask me. Nothin' else.'

"Next day when the gang saw Tanglefoot Tom swagger out on the field they thought it was some West show gone wild. He was armed to the teeth. In addition to the guns and knife which he carried the day before, he now sported a lasso coiled gracefully at his belt. But say, just as soon as the play got well started Tanglefoot had the crowd filled with admiration. Even old Doc Quackenbush, as impartial an umpire as ever called a strike, so far forgot the dignity of his position as to join in the wild cheering at some of the cowboy's marvelous plays.

"It was in the last half of the sixteenth that Tanglefoot Tom went wild. If he hadn't we wouldn't have won, I suppose, but he certainly gave us an awful scare. It happened like this. The score was 27—27, the bases were full, two were out and Bull Thompson was at the bat. Tanglefoot was dancing off third base in a reckless sort of way, when suddenly Cy Priest, the Roarer's pitcher, shot the ball

an effort to catch him napping. Tanglefoot slid
back to the bag in safety, but he seemed riled at the
very idea that any one should try to put him out.
He jumped to his feet and shook his fist threaten-
ingly at the pitcher.

" 'Oho!' he roared. 'You would try to catch me
out, would you, you horse-stealing coyote, you.
I dare you to throw it!'

"Now Cy Priest was no stenographer; no man
could dictate to him. He had just swung his arm
back to throw again when to our horror Tanglefoot
suddenly whipped out one of his guns and covered
him. The suspense was terrible. Then as the ball
left his hand there was a flash, followed by a loud
report.

" 'Was Cy killed?' we asked each other. To our
surprise and relief there he still stood; slightly
paler, perhaps, but in the same position as before,
and with the ball in his right hand ready to throw
again. The only explanation of the matter was a
small round bullet-hold in the ball. We could
scarcely believe our eyes. Again Cy Priest threw
the ball; again there was a loud report, and again

Cy found himself holding the ball in his right hand. This time there were two bullet holes in it.

"They kept at it. When Tanglefoot had emptied one gun he immediately opened fire with the other. Eleven shots were fired and then came the climax. As Cy Priest swung his arm back preparatory to his twelfth attempt the silence was awful. Then came a sudden swish, and—bang! Instantly the air was filled with flying pieces of woolen string and bits of rubber and horsehide. And from somewhere out of all this twelve little leaden pills fell and pattered cheerily upon the ground. Gentlemen, the unforeseen had happened; the ball had bust.

"As soon as the crowd had recovered from their astonishment somewhat and began to realize what had happened, they gave vent to a general sigh of relief. The baserunners jumped to their feet, the players hustled back to their positions, and Doc Quackenbush began to unwrap a new ball.

"'Not so fast thar, Mr. Umpire,' Tanglefoot Tom cried out. 'You ain't handed in yer decision yet. What's yer diagnosis of that last play, Doc?'

"The Doc was about to make some reply when he suddenly noticed that Tanglefoot was calmly reloading his guns. The Doc pulled a baseball guide from his pocket and began to thumb the pages nervously. Evidently he was unable to find any rule that just covered this particular case. He again started to speak. Tanglefoot Tom had finished loading his guns and was now fingering them tenderly. The Doc scratched his head. Then he caught sight of the bits of horsehide, rubber and woolen string that lay strewn about him, and slapped his knee joyfully. He seemed to have solved the problem.

" 'Why—er—Mr. Tanglefoot,' he said with a custom-made smile, 'there seems to be nothing in the rules that exactly applied—the fault of the rules, Mr. Tanglefoot, I assure you it's entirely the fault of the rules. But, gentlemen,' here the Doc threw out his chest and struck an attitude, 'speaking from the standpoint of a physician of considerable eminence and long standing, I feel it my painful duty— I mean my very, very pleasant duty, Mr. Tanglefoot—to pronounce that ball—why, just look at the pieces, gentlemen—of course it's a dead ball. Everybody move up a base.'

"And Tanglefoot Tom cantered home with the winning run."

XVII.

HOME RUN HANKINS SLIDES FOR HOME
SAN JUAN.

"The heaviest hitter I ever saw on any baseball team," remarked the fat ex-mascot, " was old Home Run Hankins, who held down centre field for us in the days when baseball was in its prime in Jones County. He joined the team in rather a peculiar way. It was the second game ever played between the Lightfoot Lilies and the Ringtail Roarers. Things had gone along all right until the Roarers' half of the eighth, when Bull Thompson who always was absent-minded, forgot to put his hands up to catch one of Dean Braley's swift ones. As a result the ball caught him square in the mouth, and hurried half of his front teeth down his throat. For some reason or other Bull seemed to lose his sand after that and refused positively to finish out the game. Captain Slugger Burrows called little Sammie Salmon in from centre to go behind the bat. But that left a hole in the field, and as luck would have it we had no subs. The Roarers' rooters went wild with joy. They certainly had Slugger guessing for fair. As a last resort he went up to the grandstand and called out: 'Is there any ball player in this bunch that's willing to sign with the Lightfoot Lilies for the rest of this game? I'll make it well worth his while.'

"The Roarers roared.

"But just then a frowsy, unshorn tramp, with a bleary eye and a game leg, hobbled out of the crowd and went up to the captain.

" 'Who are you?" asked Slugger.

"Again the Roarers roared.

" 'Me name's Happy Hankins,' growled the stranger, with a corrugated voice. 'I'm happy an' they call me Hankins, so—'

" 'What's your business? Can you play ball?"

" 'Well, pard, as for business, I ain't had much since oilcloth an' mattin' got fashionable. By trade I'm a journeyman carpet beater. As fur baseball

I never tried, but I think I could beat that pill one if I got de chance.'

"At that the gang let out another whoop. That got Slugger's anger up.

" 'Get out there, then,' he yelled to the tramp. 'Way out in the middle of the pasture!'

"Happy hobbled out and took his place in deep centre. He looked like a scarecrow from the grandstand, and I guess he acted as one, for not a ball had the nerve to go near him the rest of the game. He got a chance at the bat though, in the last half of the ninth. Two were gone, the bases were full, and the score stood 30—27 in favor of the Roarers. As Hankins ambled up to the plate the crowd let loose. Things certainly did look glum for us. Our only hope was that Hankins's face might scare four bad ones out of the pitcher. The first one was coming high, but to every one's surprise he stepped back and—bang! It was a moment before the crowd realized what had happened, and then the Lightfoots rose like one man and yelled as if all Bedlam had broken loose. The ball was soaring far out toward the centre field fence and the three men on bases were making for home as fast as their legs could carry them. But suddenly we noticed Hankins. He was still standing at the plate swinging his bat and swatting the air right and left.

" 'Run, you fool!' yelled Slugger Burrows from the bench. 'This ain't carpets you're beating; it's the Ringtail Roarers. Run!'

"Hankins lowered his bat and turned slowly round. He beamed upon us with a childlike smile of innocence. Then, catching sight of Slugger, he suddenly lit out for first like a startled fawn. First, second, third, he fairly flew around those bases. The ball had sailed over the fence and through the window of a shanty a hundred yards beyond. The Roarers' fielder was met at the door of the shanty by a big, husky Irishwoman with a rolling-pin and no appreciation of baseball. He returned in even more of a hurry than he had gone, but without the ball. The scorer called it 'fielder's choice.' But it mattered not; Home Run Hankins, as he was known forever after, had already crossed the plate with the winning run and the game was ours. As you can well imagine, that night, when we had returned home, he was the idol of the town. We wined him and dined him; we bought him a shave and a hair cut; we serenaded him; we did everything.

"Well, sir, Home Run made good for his new name in every game after that. As I remarked before, he was the hardest hitter I ever saw. High ones, low ones, wide ones—they were all the same to him as long as they came swift enough. If the pitcher tried to fool him with a slow one he'd swing his bat the wrong way and drive the ball up against the catcher. I've seen him knock out three men in one game with that stunt. Not satisfied with being able to connect with the ball himself he undertook to give the rest of the team instructions. Any quiet afternoon every man of the Lightfoot Lilies could be seen lined up in front of a long row of carpets, beating them for dear life under the careful supervision of Home Run Hankins. As soon as the boys had developed sufficient force by this means he began to rack his brain for some method of teaching accuracy.

"He finally got hold of one of those new-fangled

pitching cannons, and for a time that did the trick to perfection. The team got so proficient with the stick that batting practice went off like clock-work. First there'd be a little puff of smoke, then a loud report, and a second afterward the batter'd be tearing 'round the bases while the ball was trying to find a resting place on the other side of the fence. The neighbors kicked at the noise, but we couldn't hear 'em as long as it did the team any good. The reason we finally quit the scheme was that the rainstorms brought on by the concussions of the cannon compelled us to cancel over half our games on account of wet grounds.

"But, like many other great men, Hankins met his Waterloo at last through the demon rum. We argued with him time and again, but all to no purpose. 'Does it make any difference in my batting?' he would ask. We had to admit that it didn't. When he got so bad that he saw double, he'd aim in between the two balls, and home runs, three-baggers and doubles materialized with the same old regularity. The cause of his downfall was far worse than that.

"It was in the annual game with the Ringtail Roarers, just one year after he first joined the team. Again it was the last half of the ninth inning, with the bases full and two out; again the score stood 30—27 in favor of the Roarers, and again Happy Hankins was to the bat. But this time he was not greeted with jeers; the Roarers were filled with dread. Hankins reeled to the plate with an unsteady gait, but his eye was still with him. He drove the first ball pitched through the same old window in the same old shanty. The men on bases dashed for home and the Lightfoot crowd went wild. But their mirth was suddenly cut short and despair filled their hearts. Hankins, who had been zig-zagging his way around the bases, made an extra lunge to one side just as he reached third. At that the umpire turned on his heel and cried, 'Out for running out of base line! The Roarers win!'

"Next day Hankins naturally had remorse. He swore he'd never touch a ball again. He turned a deaf ear to all our entreaties and promises of forgiveness and shortly afterward disappeared from town. From that time on I never heard of him until the war with Spain, when I read in the *Jones County Courier* that he had enlisted. Poor old Home Run! He lost his life at San Juan Hill. The very first cannon shot brought back memories of the good old baseball days when we practised batting with the pitching cannon. Instinctively he seized the barrel of his gun, made a vicious swing at the air and started off hot-foot toward the enemy. He breathed his last while sliding for a Spanish block house. Poor old Home Run!"

The fat ex-mascot sighed feelingly as he brushed a hot tear from his cheek. His listeners respected his grief and were silent.

XVIII.

THE FOOTE TWINS BREAK UP BASEBALL
IN JONES COUNTY

"**O**ne of the prettiest games of baseball I've ever seen," remarked the fat man who was at one time mascot for the Lightfoot Lilies, "was the last game played between the Ringtail Roarers and the Lightfoot Lilies. It ended with an unfortunate misunderstanding, however, that put further games between the two teams out of the question, and to this day there have only been two men who could say positively which team was in the right. Those two men were the Foote twins, who played right and left fields, respectively, for the Lightfoots. The two Foote twins were mates if ever two feet were, and that's what caused all the trouble. 'Left' Foote, as we called the one who held down left field, wasn't much at the bat, but 'Right' Foote was a holy terror. For that reason, Captain Slugger Burrows always placed their names pretty far apart on the batting list, so that one never came to bat while the other was on base. So you see, if the game was close, he could have 'Right' Foote bat twice, and on account of the brothers' extraordinary resemblance, the opposing team would never spot the change. It was a sort of a case of the captain's putting his best Foote forward in tight places.

"The Roarers must have got wise about the trick, for the afternoon of the big game their captain came to Slugger Burrows and said that unless the Footes were placed within two of each other on the batting list, he'd withdraw his team from the field. Although this demand was out of accordance with all rules of the game, Slugger didn't want to disappoint the big crowds that had come from all over Jones County to see the contest, and gave in.

"Cy Priest was in the box for the Roarers, and that meant work for us if we expected to win. The Roarers had a noisy bunch of rooters on hand, and they tried their hardest to rattle us with a new-fangled song they'd got hold of. It went something like this:

> " *'You're quite a daisy,*
> *But you have your faults.*
> *Your 'Right' Foote is lazy*
> *Your 'Left' Foote is crazy.*
> *Oh, please do be aisy*
> *An' we'll teach you to waltz'*

"But it took more than vaudeville talk to phase the Lightfoot Lilies in those days, and when we came to the bat in the last half of the ninth the score stood tied at 17—17. Bull Thompson, the first man up, flied out to centre. Then the captain called 'Foote to the bat,' and the gang loosened up. We had a hunch that 'Right' Foote would be the one to toe the plate, and when a moment later the batter connected for three bags to deep left we had no doubt as to his identity. For the next five minutes Jones County made Rome sound like Prohibition Park on the howling business. The other Foote turned handsprings all the way to third base and started coaching in a way that would have put a woman's debating society to shame. Sam Strong

put a damper on the enthusiasm, however, by foul-
ing out on the first ball pitched. The two Footes
began to whisper earnestly on third and the crowd
was silent in suspense. 'The other Foote to the bat,'
Captain Slugger Burrows shouted. The Foote on
the coaching line at third jogged slowly in until he
was about five yards from the plate. Then with a
sudden sprint, before the people realized what had
happened, he dashed across the rubber. 'Hurrah!'
he cried, waving his hands wildly above his head,
'I'm the Foote that made the hit! We've won; they're
it!' The teams rushed in from the field and the po-
lice force couldn't have controlled the crowd if he'd
tried. The other team rushed up and protested, but
even at that all would have been well if one of the
Footes—either one—had only kept quiet. They
were both jumping up and down yelling 'I'm the
Foote that made the hit! I'm "Right" Foote, he's
"Left"!' Soon they got fighting as to which was
which and every one jumped down from the stands
and joined in. Each of the Footes claimed that he
had made the hit and then scored while the other
was coaching. The Roarers said they had no proof

that the one who scored was the one who made the hit, and that the Footes had batted out of order anyway. The Lightfoots claimed that some one had won the game for them and said they didn't care who. We tried to appeal to the umpire, but he had sifted through the gate when the rough-house first broke out.

"Well, as I said, that broke up the games between the Ringtail Roarers and the Lightfoot Lilies, and to this day we don't know how the last game came out. Some people lay it to jealousy between the Foote twins, but to me that seems unfair. You see they looked so much alike that each might easily have mistaken the other for himself."

XIX.

THE LILIES WIN BY A SIXTEENTH OF A RUN.

"Three to two a close game?"

The fat ex-mascot sniffed contemptuously.

"Why, back in the days when I was connected with the Lightfoot Lilies we had contests that were so close they fairly stifled. Take the Jones County championship of '86 for example.

"In the final game we defeated the formidable Ringtail Roarers by a score of 1-16 to 0. Now that was close.

"Impossible, you say? Not at all. This fractional score was made possible by the mathematical precision of the decisions rendered by that prince of all umpires, old Doc Quackenbush.

"Cy Priest was pitching for the home team and it's only just to say right here that even if he was a

Ringtail Roarer he was probably the speediest twirler that ever shot the pill over the pie. Why he pitched so fast that an ordinary umpire had to keep his eyes wide open to see the ball go by, let alone being able to tell whether it went over the plate or not.

"From the bleachers you couldn't even tell he was pitching except for the fact that the catcher tossed the ball back to him at regular intervals. Well, anyhow, that's the man who was pitching for the Roarers.

"The scoring was all done in the beginning of the first inning. Bull Thompson, our heavy hitting backstop, selected a well-seasoned log of lignum vitae from among the Lilies' bats and swaggered to the plate.

"As he doffed his cap in response to the deafening applause that greeted him the rasping sound of tearing flannel rent the air and an abnormally developed biceps burst through his right shirt sleeve. Bull Thompson was in prime condition in '86.

"Cy Priest hitched his trousers and drew his arm

back. Bull swung his bat defiantly. Zip! came the ball. Crack! went the bat against it, and a moment later a cloud of dust was chasing the Bull toward first.

" 'Hurray, he's safe!' shouted the Lily rooters as the Bull crossed first well before the ball reached there.

" 'Safe nothin'; he's out!' cried the Roarers, springing to their feet and pointing to the shortstop, who had just gobbled in a fly that seemed to have come from the Bull's bat.

"We couldn't understand it; were there two balls?

"Doc Quackenbush rushed over and examined the ball that the shortstop had just caught. Then he ran over to first and grabbed the ball which the first baseman was trying to hide. A smile of intelligence illumined his face.

" 'Ladies and gentlemen,' he began, addressing the grandstands, 'a most unusual problem has presented itself to me in my official capacity of umpire. Mr. Thompson hit the ball so hard that he split it in two pieces. Half of it was caught on the fly. The other half he beat out to first. After a careful diagnosis of the case the only just decision, I believe, is to declare Mr. Thompson half out at first.'

"At the unusual solution of the case a general buzz of excitement broke out all over the field.

" 'Then make the half of him that's out get off the base,' demanded Cy Priest, who was captain of the Roarers. 'I object to—'

" 'Pardon me,' Doc Quackenbush interrupted 'I did not say half of the runner was all out; I said all of the runner was half out. Therefore—'

" 'Hi, there! He's making for second!' the Roarers yelled. 'Throw the ball! Quick!'

"They looked around just in time to see the shortstop clap his half of the ball on the Bull as the latter was sliding for second.

" 'Well, he's all out now, anyhow,' Cy said.

"But the Bull evidently thought otherwise, for the next instant he had picked himself up and was tearing toward third. The shortstop, all excitement, slung the half ball he had over to the third basement, and the Bull was once more touched out. In the meantime Doc Quackenbush had taken out his pencil and was making lightning calculations on his cuff.

" 'What in the name of Simplicity Jefferson are you doing now?' demanded Cy, turning on the umpire. 'Do you mean to say that that man isn't out yet?'

" 'He is exactly seven-eighths out at present,' the Doc replied calmly. 'He still has one-eighth to the good.'

" 'What do you think we are playing, anyway? Baseball or arithmetic?'

" 'Come here, and I'll prove it for you.'

"The Doc pulled up his other sleeve and began figuring on that cuff.

" 'Half out at first,' he began. 'Remaining half put half out at second, ½ of ½ making ¼. This ¼ makes for third where it is again reduced ½, leaving but ⅛, and there goes that eighth, by jingo!'

"True enough, Bull Thompson, still one-eighth to the good, was sprinting for home as if his mother-in-law was after him. The third baseman socked the half ball which he had down to the catcher.

" 'Throw your half, too, you dummy!' Cy yelled

to the first baseman.

"The two half balls reached the catcher almost together. He caught the one from third and thumped Bull on the back with it. The throw from first was high, however, and as the catcher jumped for it, the Bull, still one-sixteenth to the good, dived under him and crossed the plate with what finally proved to be the winning run.

"For proof of all this you have only to visit Jones County, as I understand that the shirt upon which Doc Quackenbush made his remarkable calculations is still preserved in the trophy case at the town hall."

THE END.

THE FAT EX-MASCOT.

In 1907, the author, Robert Rudd Whiting, published another book of his typically tall tales. In the book were three more baseball stories with an additional nine tales all of them set in the home of that great baseball team, the Lightfoot Lilies, of Oxendale, in Jones County.

The title of the book—*A Ball of Yarn, Its Unwinding*—indicates the thrust of the chapters, that aren't called "chapters" but "skeins", a sensible switch since we are reading about A BALL OF **YARN!**

These yarns or tall tales are told by a small group of friends, windy spinners all, who are sitting around a stove in the hotel owned by one of the participants, 360 pound William Little (!) who says...but let the massive Bill Little begin this session—or stretch—of *A Ball of Yarn—Its Unwinding.*

Slid down the frozen stream to friends and safety below.

THE YARN OF THE INVENTIVE VAMP.

The First Skein

June bugs darted through the open windows of the Mansion House and butted drunkenly against the tin reflectors of the kerosene lamps along the office walls. The monotonous buzzing from the fly-paper on the desk was from time to time reinforced by the frantic protests of some new victim.

Four pairs of legs radiated from the cold stove in the center of the room: the massive, imposing legs that supported the three hundred and sixty-odd pounds of William Little, landlord of the Mansion House; the long, literary legs that terminated in Ezra Norton, editor of The Oxendale Townsman; the sophisticated, urban legs, enwrapped in startling checks and capped with patent leather, which hustled, when called upon, for

Lochinvar Leary, the cigar drummer; and, finally, the legs inside the earth-encrusted boots that had the honor of upholding Ebenezer Abbott, Oxendale's sage and raconteur.

Mr Little laid down the paper with which he had been fanning himself, and mopped his ample brow.

"It's hot," he announced feelingly.

"It is hot," admitted Ebenezer Abbott, "but it might be worse."

"Might be worse!" gasped Mr. Leary. "Why, if 'twas any hotter than this, them flies over there would drown in their own perspiration."

"I say it might be worse," repeated Mr. Abbott calmly. "It might be cold. An' fur downright peskiness, hot weather ain't in th' same thermometer with a right smart cold snap. Why, I remember oncet it wus so everlastin' cold right here in Oxendale thet there warn't man, woman nor child in th' whole durned town thet wus able t' find where he lived fur more'n six hours. An' 'twould 've been longer'n thet if Jedge Poor's house hadn't been destroyed through a fortunate piece of carelessness on his part. What did th' cold weather have t' do *with it? I'll tell ye."*

And the Sage of Oxendale thereupon unfolded—

The Yarn of the Breath-Bound Village

'T WUS about nine o'clock in th' mornin' when I started down toward th' post office, an' say, mebbe it warn't cold! Why, ye could see yer breath so durn plain thet—wal, I'll tell ye jest how durn plain ye could see yer breath.

About half way down th' hill I seed Si Draper comin' outer his gate. He wus puffin' out big clouds of cold breath, too.

"Mornin' Si," says I.

"Mornin' yerself," says Si. "Hold yer breath a minute so's I ken see who ye be. Oh, it's you, Eb, is it? I thought so from th' sound of yer voice. Phew! but it's cold!"

Say, thet there "phew!" of Si's gave rise to a cold-breath cloud thet fur ten minutes completely surrounded us.

Jest as it wus clearin' away we saw another cloud comin' right fur us, an' a-fore we had time t' dodge, we bumped plum inter old Jedge Poor an' sent him sprawlin'.

I knew it were th' jedge from th' words he gave utterance to at th' time of th' bump.

Wal, sir, Jedge Poor wus so winded from his fall, an' spluttered an' panted so, thet a-fore we'd finished explainin' to him how it all happened, we wus all three a-shiverin' in th' midst of an impenetrable cold-breath fog.

It wus so thick thet y' couldn't see yer hand in front of yer face, even when ye held it there.

We groped around quite a spell a-fore we finally found each other. Then we grabbed hold of hands an' decided t' stick t'gether till things cleared up some.

"Now then, all t'gether," commanded Si. "Hold yer breaths!"

We all held.

But jest as th' air began t' thin out a mite, th' jedge, whose face had been gettin' redder 'n redder, couldn't hold in no longer, an' exploded with a breath thet clouded us in denser'n ever.

We tried it again an' again, but 'twarn't no use. Th' jedge always exploded jest at th' critical moment when we were beginnin' t' see our way out, an' every time he did, th' fog closed in thicker'n before.

So we quit thet plan an' decided t' try an' get somewheres. We grabbed hold of coat-tails an' started in t' feel our way as best we could.

But arter we'd been crawlin' along fur about fifteen minutes we found we'd been doin' nothin' but goin' round in circles an' hadn't got nowheres. What's more, we wuz all pantin' so hard from th' exertion an' excitement thet our breathclouds thickened th' fog almost t' suffication.

Say, you've never been lost in yer own breath, right in yer native town, shiverin' almost t' death, but feared t' move fur fear of gettin' more lost, have ye? Wal, then, ye can't comprehend th' awful despair an' helplessness of it. Words can't express it.

Fur a few minutes we jest stood there a-tremblin', too durn terrorfied t' do anything.

Then, as if by one impulse, we all threw back our

heads an' shouted at th' top of our lungs:

"Help! Help! Help! Help!"

Gosh all hemlock! how we must've hollered! Least wise every man, woman an' child in Oxendale, 1,876 souls includin' Ovid Phelps who ain't got any soul accordin' t' th' parson, came rushin' outer their houses t' see what wuz th' trouble with who.

As fast as they'd come, why, of course, they'd get lost in their breaths, too. 'Twarn't long a-fore th' whole population wuz runnin' 'round like chickens with their heads off, bumpin' inter each other, an' a-swearin' out more fog at every bump. 'Twus awful.

Goodness only knows what would've happened if it hadn't been fur thet carelessness on th' part of Jedge Poor.

Ye see when he kem out he left th' candle burnin' on th' cupboard right next t' th' matches. When th' candle burned down, th' matches started up, an' pretty soon th' whole durn house wus a-fire from top t' bottom.

It hadn't been burnin' more'n an hour a-fore th' air begun t' thaw, an' by th' time th' roof fell in, th' fog had melted away so 's we could all see where we lived.

The whole town immediately stopped their cussin' an' broke out in one mighty cheer.

Course 'twus kinder hard on th' jedge, losin' his house thet way, but we all chipped in an' built him a better one.

Not thet th' fire weren't all his own fault, mind ye, but—wal, if *his* house hadn't burned down we'd a-probably spent all th' rest of thet winter gropin' around in a cold-breath fog tryin' t' find *our* houses.

"Why, that must have been the winter that the druggist's cows all gave cold cream" suggested the landlord with an ill-concealed wink at the cigar drummer.

Mr. Abbott glared at him fiercely.

"All joking aside, though," mused Ezra Norton, "it certainly was an unusually cold winter."

"What do you know about it?" snapped Mr. Abbott, jealous of sharing his own particular winter with anybody else. "Thet winter, young man, took place a-fore you were born."

"I've often heard my grandfather speak of it,"

continued the editor, unperturbed. "And while your account of what transpired while the breath-fog was at its densest is substantially correct, you have omitted the interesting detail of how Judge Poor's widowed mother was snatched from the jaws of death at the eleventh hour."

"Umph!" sneered the sage. "I'd like t' know what in tarnation yer grandfather knew about it."

"Grandfather," replied the editor with great dignity, "was Captain of the Oxendale Volunteer Hose Company, sworn fire-fighters, and I have this from his own lips."

Whereupon Mr. Norton unwound—

The Yarn of the Inventive Vamp

THE instant the fog had cleared away sufficiently for Grandfather to see that the judge's house was ablaze, he rallied his brave fire laddies about him. In spite of the fact that they had over half a mile further to go, they reached the scene of the conflagration almost simultaneously with the hook-and-ladder company.

By that time the unusual hubbub about the place had aroused the judge's aged mother from her afternoon nap on the top floor. She rushed to the nearest window and screamed piercingly for help.

"Don't jump!" the men of the hook-and-ladder company warned her. "We'll have a ladder up in less 'n no time."

But try as they would they could not budge the ladder from the truck; it had frozen fast. A groan of horror swept through the crowd. The old lady wrung her hands piteously.

'Twas then that Grandfather stepped into the breach.

"Rest easy, madam," he called in stentorian tones. "I will find a way."

He had observed that the water froze just as fast as it left the nozzle. It was to this observation of Grandfather's that the aged lady owed her life. He played the hose against the top-story window and she slid down the frozen stream to friends and safety below.

As the editor finished, Ebenezer Abbott gave a snort of disgust. Then, apropos of nothing apparently, he observed: "George Washin'ton must've been chock full o' lies. Leastwise, accordin' to all reports, he never managed t' work any off."

"Well, of course cold weather's got its disadvantages," put in Mr. Leary, for the sake of peace, "but I don't think it's as bad as weather like this under any circumstances. There ain't so many bad smells around when it's cold."

"Heat undoubtedly does intensify odors," agreed the landlord. "I've often noticed it, especially in the case of Blinksey Black, the famous outfielder of the old Lightfoot Lilies who held the baseball championship of Jones County for so many years. Early in the spring when the afternoons were still crisp he used to have considerable trouble in judging difficult fly balls, but when the season advanced and the weather got real good and blistery, he was better than most ball-players who had the use of their eyesight."

"Huh?" questioned the bewildered cigar drummer. "You say he was better than most players that

had the use of their eyesight? Well, how in the name of a Russian general could he play ball at all if he couldn't see? It may be that I'm suffering from the heat, but somehow or other I don't seem to be in quite right on your conversation."

"Why, Blinksey Black, the blind ballplayer of the Lightfoot Lilies—you've surely heard of him if you follow sporting matters at all?"

As Mr. Leary was not quite sure, there was nothing left for Landlord Little but to relate—

The Yarn of the Blind Ball-Tosser

BLACK had been with the Lilies two or three seasons when one day some jealous woman who'd mistaken him for another man suddenly gave him the carbolic sling and he lost the use of both eyes. Now, you'd naturally think that that would have meant his finish as a ball-player, but it didn't.

Have you ever noticed how when a man loses the use of a leg, or something, the strength that was in that leg always goes to some other part of his body? Why, take some of these skinny little armless guys you see; they have underpinnings on 'em that Samson needn't have been ashamed of before he had his hair cut.

Well, that's the way it was with Black. When he lost his eyesight it went to his nose. He developed a sense of smell that would have brought tears of envy to the eyes of the finest bloodhound that ever sniffed a scent.

We discovered that at practice one day. Black was standing close by listening to the batting when a wild pitch made straight for him.

"Look out!" we yelled.

But Black, to our amazement, instead of dodging, threw up his hands and gobbled in the ball as easy as you please.

"I thought I smelled 'er coming," he explained. "Violets, isn't it?" he added with a sniff.

We couldn't figure out what he meant until Bull Thompson, the catcher, shamefaced and blushing, admitted that he had washed his hands with scented soap that morning. A slight perfume had clung to the ball, and Black had smelled out its course.

"By the great Dan Brouthers!" exclaimed Slugger Burrows, the Lilies' captain. "There's no reason why you should give up baseball, Blinksey. Report for practise in your old place in left-field tomorrow."

Black did report; and, say, would you believe it, he was as good a fielder as ever he'd been before his accident. A single drop of heliotrope placed on the ball in the first inning was enough to make him follow it around like a hound all the rest of the game.

At the bat he was ever better than he'd been before. His keen sense of smell enabled him to tell which way the ball was twisting the moment it left the pitcher's hand, and he always knew exactly what curve to expect.

The one thing that troubled us about Blinksey for a time was his base-running. We first tried spraying heliotrope along the base line. That would work all right for a few innings, but after the ball had been batted around the diamond a bit, he was likely to run afoul of grounder trails. When he did he was just as apt as not to leave his course suddenly and dart out to center-field on some false scent.

It was Bull Thompson who finally solved the problem. While we still stuck to the heliotrope for the ball perfume, we substituted a powerful essence of white rose as a base-line spray. This worked to perfection, and save for a few days when he had a slight cold in his head, there wasn't a better base-runner on the team than Blinksey Black.

But, like most great men, Black had his downfall. And, as luck would have it, it came just when it would be most felt.

'Twas in the last inning of the great contest with the Ringtail Roarers for the championship of Jones County. The Lilies were leading, 12-10, and although the Roarers had the bases filled, two were out.

On the third ball pitched, the batter drove a long, low fly to left. We started to reach for our hats. Blinksey's nose had never failed us yet.

But this time the unexpected happened. Just as Black was stretching forth his hands to receive the ball, some well-meaning but misguided admirer threw a bouquet at him.

William Little, Landloard of the Mansion House.

An agonized expression of indecision came over Blinksey's face. He hesitated. The pungent perfume of the freshly picked flowers was too much for him. He dived wildly at the flying bouquet, the men on bases cantered home, and the game was lost.

But that wasn't all. The ball struck Black on the nose and broke it. His stock in trade as a baseball-player was ruined for ever afterward.

If then he'd only had the acute sense of hearing that he developed as soon as his nose was broken, he'd undoubtedly have detected the difference in sound between the ball and the bouquet and might be playing the game today.

Tender memories that he had awakened within himself forced a heavy sigh from deep down in the landlord's bosom.

"Truth is certainly stranger than fiction," commented the editor.

"Mebbe so," muttered Ebenezer Abbott, reaching for his hat and coat. "Mebbe so. There's no denyin' thet thet wus strange, though,—no matter how ye choose t' take it."

The Second Skein

"It's a little cooler than last night, Mr. Abbott."

This was the cigar drummer's third attempt to draw the Sage of Oxendale into conversation.

"What's the matter with you, Eb?" demanded the portly landlord. "You ain't yourself tonight. There must be something on your mind."

"There is," admitted Mr. Abbott, reluctantly. "My conscience has been a-troublin' me all evenin'. D'ye remember thet double-tailed pointer dog thet I exhibited at th' county fair several years ago?"

The landlord and the editor nodded non-committingly.

"Wal, th' whole thing wus an out-'n-out fake. Thet pointer warn't a two-tailed dog at all."

A murmur of polite surprise greeted this con-

fession.

"It's kinder been weighin' on my conscience ever since," he continued, "an' now I'm goin' t' tell th' truth about it an' get it off my mind fur good an' all."

Whereupon he unburdened himself of—

The Yarn of the Two-tailed Pointer

WHAT thet two-tailed dog of mine really wus wus a one-tailed dog with his tail split in two halves. I bred him myself and I oughter know.

His father and mother were th' two finest durn critters thet ever pointed a bird, so 'twus only natural thet he should've been a hunter right from th' start.

Th' thing thet tempted me t' stoop t' deceivin' the county fair happened th' very first time I took him gunnin'. Th' second he laid eyes on a bird his tail stiffened out like a ramrod.

But he seemed to be in awful agony over somethin'. His tail swelled up an' begun t' quiver an' tremble like it wus almost fit to bust with agitation.

Suddenly th' tip seemed to open up a little, an' then,—swish! His tail had split clean down th' whole length.

I couldn't figure it out ontil I noticed thet th' tarnation pup was cross-eyed. Y' see he'd been tryin' t' point th' bird th' way it looked t' him.

"Hope your conscience feels better," said Mr. Leary, rather doubtfully.

"Speaking of the county fair reminds me," Editor Ezra Norton hastily interposed, "the circus is coming to town next month. I had a letter from the advance agent this morning. And, by the way, he ought to be here himself sometime tonight to see about bill-posters, show-cards and other literature. He asked me to engage a room for him."

"What did he write to you for?" demanded Landlord Little, indignantly, "Who does he think's running this hotel, anyway? That's what I'd like to know."

"Why—er—you see, he had to write to me about advertising space in The Townsman, *and I sup-*

pose—"

"Don't see what he wants to advertise in The Townsman *for. Nobody ever reads it. And even if they did—"*

"Here comes a hack from the 8:15," interrupted the cigar drummer, who had detected a rumbling of wheels. "Maybe this is him now."

The hack drew up outside. Murphy, the driver, stuck his head in the door and slid a suit-case across the floor. A few seconds later the owner of it entered.

He was a little man whose artfulness in dress and toilet gave him an impression of prosperity that was not borne out by closer scrutiny. The wondrous curl of his mustaches distracted attention from a two days' growth of beard on his chin; the dazzling stone in his shirt-front blinded the eye to the grease-spots on his waistcoat, his gilded watch-chain delayed one's discovery of the fact that his coat was shiny at the elbows, while the pearl-colored gaiters that overshadowed the shabbiness of his shoes were equally effective in diverting observation from the frayed spots on the bottoms of his trousers.

The arrival glanced inquiringly at the group

around the stove.

"Can I get a room here? I'm Mr. Sinclair—Mr. D'Arcy Sinclair of Ring Brothers' Stupendous Circus and Educational Side Show, one ring, children half-price, greatest—"

"We were expecting you, Mr. Sinclair,' said Landlord Little, rising ponderously, and taking the newcomer's suit-case. "If you'll follow me upstairs I'll show you your room. You were lucky to strike us right in our dull season."

The satellites of the stove smoked in silence until the return of the landlord. They waited expectantly while he lowered himself into his chair.

"Wal?" suggested Mr. Abbott.

"He'll be down in a minute," Mr. Little announced. "He'll be here tomorrow night, too."

"Excuse me, Mr. Landlord," said Mr. D'Arcy Sinclair, making his reappearance a few minutes later, "but can you tell me whether I'd be apt to find the editor of The Townsman *in his office this time o' night?"*

"Why, here he is right here," said Mr. Little, indicating the editor with a wave of his hand.

"*From the way he spoke I thought he knew you. Mr. Norton, shake hands with Mr. Sinclair. Draw up a chair, sir.*"

They edged around to make room for another pair of feet on the stove.

"*I'll only keep you a minute, Mr. Norton,*" the Circus man assured him. "*Have you pencil and paper about you? Good. I am going to put you in possession of material for a news article of tremendous importance, which I know you will be glad to make room for on the first page of your esteemed journal. Perhaps, in the interests of the Circus, I should withhold these facts for the present, but conscience is an awful thing, gentlemen, and in this case it clearly shows me that my duty to the public outweighs my duty to my employers.*

"*While it is true that any announcement in the public prints of the illness of the Human Louvre, our tattooed man, will undoubtedly keep thousands away from the side show of Ring Brothers' Stupendous Circus, yet—yet, gentlemen, in view of the remarkable nature of the illness of this abnormally athletic, astoundingly accomplished* and *absorbingly artistic acquisition, it seems unjust to the best interests of science to withhold—"*

"Tattooed man sick, eh?" ventured Mr. Abbott. "What's th' trouble with him?"

By way of reply Mr. Sinclair unfolded the facts of—

The Yarn of the Human Louvre

T ATTOOED men are hard to handle. I suppose it's the artisticness of their temperaments—too much imagination. The better they are, the worse their imaginations. And our tattooed man was the best in the business.

You surely have heard of him if you follow the fine arts at all. The Human Louvre was his stage alias, and leading connoisseurs have assured me that his pictures were possessed of a certain life and color that is lacking in many of the finest specimens in the equally famous Louvre in Paris.

Aside from the finest galaxy of needle-and-ink sketches that artist ever put on cuticle, the Human

Louvre had a chest expansion that required an elastic skin to hold it all.

And he used that same expansion to marvelous effect in exhibiting the two *chef d'oeuvres* that adorned his manly chest.

One of these masterpieces was a magnificent specimen of Chinese dragon in red, yellow, and blue; the other, a splendid red, blue and green South African lion, rampant *and* roaring.

The two were pictured facing each other, with their heads about four inches apart. By sharply expanding and contracting his chest, the Human Louvre could give the dragon and lion the appearance of springing at each other in a way that inspired our patrons with mingled anxiety, awe *and* admiration.

Marvelous, you say? Never anything like it. But just as the world's greatest savants, philosophers and literati were about to sit up and take notice, Daisy the Fat Lady cast her shadow across his path.

Now, what under the sun an art amateur like the Human Louvre could see in Daisy the Fat Lady is beyond me. She was of a shallow, superficial nature, incapable of appreciating art in any form, and she had a figure that took fifty-seven seconds to pass a given point.

But fall in love with her he did. She, as might be expected, took a violent fancy to the glass-eater, a shiftless, good-for-nothing sort of fellow.

Well, that started the Human Louvre on his downward course. He took to mooning and sulking until he actually began to worry himself thin.

He grew more peaked and tired-looking every day until finally, at the end of the week, he came to me and said:

"Boss, I'm in a bad way."

"Oh, never mind Daisy," I urged him cheerfully. "You're too good for her, anyway."

" 'Tain't Daisy," he mournfully replied. I'm getting so awful thin, though, that—"

"Forget it, " I told him. "What if you are falling off a bit? Look at the living skeleton; he's happy."

" 'Tain't the getting thin so much, boss. It's the results. Have you noticed the dragon and the lion on my chest lately? They used to be a good four inches apart, but I've been losing flesh so that there's only two inches between 'em now.

"Now, it may be just my imagination, but somehow it seems to me that that dragon's fang is curled a little tighter and that the lion's mouth is open just a mite wider than it used to be.

"I know they're only pictures and all that, but I can't help worrying a good deal about it just the same. Supposing I should get so awful thin that them beasts would be right on top of one another and get to scrapping? Why, say, boss, sometimes when I get to thinking about it in the middle of the night, it just strings cold sweat beads all up and down my backbone."

Now what do you think of that for the working of an artistic imagination? I told him to take cod-liver oil and to drink plenty of ale, and that before he knew it he'd have so much chest that that lion and Chinese dragon would be backing into each other 'round behind his shoulder-blades.

But he kept right on worrying and worrying, and in spite of the cod-liver oil and ale, he worried himself so thin that the week following, when he took his seat on the platform, there was scarcely a quarter of an inch between the dragon's head and the lion's mouth.

All during the lectures that day he seemed to be acting strangely. Every once in a while he'd start suddenly as though terrified at something. Then he'd glance nervously at his chest.

Next day he didn't show up. I went to see him and found him sick in bed. He was breathing with great difficulty. His landlady said that he'd been complaining of terrible pains in the chest ever since morning.

"The doctor says it's pneumonia," she told me. "He says he ought to be taken to the hospital."

When she had left the room the poor old Human Louvre beckoned to me to come close.

"Say," he said in a hoarse whisper, "don't you think you'd be complaining of sharp pains if you had a rough-house on your chest like this?"

With a sickly smile he unbuttoned his nightshirt and bared his chest.

I gave one look and drew back aghast.

The lion had the dragon's head in its mouth, and—it may have been due to the sick man's labored breathing—but it certainly seemed as if that lion was slowly chewing up that dragon.

Pneumonia? Maybe. But whatever it is they'll have to keep his mind from worrying, and fatten him up enough to pull them beasts apart again. If they don't, that lion will get that Chinese dragon and the poor old Human Louvre along with it.

What became of Daisy the Fat Lady? Oh, she married the glass-eater. But they hadn't been housekeeping three days before he kicked on her cooking and ate up her ruby necklace, to say nothing of nibbling most of the settings out of her diamond rings. Served her good and right, too.

"Humph. I don't see as how a yarn like thet's a-goin' t' keep folks from attendin' th' Circus," observed the Sage of Oxendale. *"I never did take much stock in them fool tattooed men, anyway. When I wanter look at pictures I want 'em in a book where I can turn 'em over t' suit m'self."*

"Really?" said Mr. Sinclair more hopefully. *"It does me a world of good to hear you say so."*

"What I wanter see when I go t' th' Circus," con-

tinued Mr. Abbott, "is th' Circassian girl, th' fat lady, th'—did y' say thet th' glass-eater was still with ye?"

The Circus man's face clouded again.

"Dear, dear," he sighed mournfully. "I'd almost forgotten about that. No, we fired the glass-eater that eloped with the fat lady and engaged another one—but he's sick too. Splendid artist in every respect, as long as he stuck to a simple plate-glass diet. But on his birthday, his fellow artists went and gave him a sumptuous banquet with a magnificent stained-glass window representing "The Temptation of St. Anthony" for the piece de resistance. The food proved too rich for him and not only upset his stomach but developed a sort of dual personality in him as well. Every once in a while the Temptation side of him would get making flirt-eyes at the Circassian girl. Then, without the slightest warning, the St. Anthony side of his nature would get the upper hand and he'd have remorse so bad that he'd have to start in on a two weeks' fast to discipline himself. Now far be it from the Circus management, gentlemen, to interfere with any man's *religion, but when a glass-eater refuses to eat, he ain't any longer a glass eater. So we had to let him go too."*

"Is that for publication, too?" inquired Mr. Norton, arranging his notes.

Mr. Sinclair thoughtfully scratched his chin.

"Why, yes," he finally decided. "I don't see any harm in your printing it as long as you don't use my name. Be sure to keep me out of it, though. Some people would be just mean enough to think that I was using a man's affliction to advertise the show."

"Say," said Lochinvar Leary, "I've been thinkin' about that human tattooed man of yours. Now there's a case where I should think all this faith-cure-mental-suggestion business would have the bulge on medicine."

" 'Twould," declared Mr. Abbott before the circus man had time to answer.

"Ah, then you know of a case, sir, where men-tal—er—suggestion was successfully employed?" ventured Mr. Sinclair.

"Wal, not exactly," admitted Mr. Abbott, "but

it's a poor rule thet don't work both ways, an' if this here mental business can kill a fine, strong, healthy man in th' prime of life, I don't see why it shouldn't be able t' cure an ailin' man thet's gradu'ly wastin' away. Ezra, d'ye remember hearin' tell of Si Marland's death when you wus a boy?"

"Seems to me I do," replied the editor.

"Dropped dead at his birthday party. Heart disease, wasn't it?

"Nope. Thet's what th' doctors said, but they wus wrong. 'Twas old age."

"Old age!" exclaimed Mr. Norton. "Why, he was only 45 when he died!"

Instead of making a direct reply, Mr. Abbot related—

The Yarn of Suggestive Senility

WHEN Si Marland wus 47 years old—*not* 45, Ezra—he gave th' finest durn birthday party thet wus ever held in Oxendale. He had a special barrel of Connecticut greenin's sent up

jest fur th' apple toddy, an' all day long while
Si an' his company wus emptyin' one crock,
there'd be another one brewin' t' take its place.

Now Si Marland's apple toddy warn't like ordinary apple toddy. Josh Long always used t' say thet
if it had been Si's apple toddy thet had made Adam
fall, he could've understood it better. It wus potent.
Y' mightn't notice it so much at first, but then, all
of a sudden, while 'twus still tingling 'round in yer
finger-tips, 'twould shoot down an' tangle up th'
steerin' geer in yer legs a'fore y' knowed it.

Consequence wus, when Si an' his friends sat
down t' th' birthday feast thet night—wal, they wus
consid'rably under th' influence.

Things would've been all right at thet if old Mrs.
Marland hadn't baked a big birthday cake with 47
lighted candles in it an' set it down in front of Si
jest as th' toddy wus makin' itself most felt.

Si straightened up an' stared at thet cake. He
seemed sorter suprised at something. He rubbed his
eyes an' looked again. He began t' turn white an'
then, all at once, he threw both hands t' his chest
an' fell over backwards.

Ebenezer Abbott, Oxendale's Sage and Raconteur.
157

Wal, *you* know what th' doctors said. Old Doc Chapman who got there first said 'twus heart desease, an' Doc Phelps arterwards agreed with him.

But I know better. Josh Long, who was settin' right next t' Si, told me 'twas nothin' of th' sort. He said that th' apple toddy had made Si see double. Consequence wus, when he saw them 47 candles in thet there cake he counted 94 of 'em an' jest dropped off natur'ly from old age. Josh was cock sure about it because he remembers perfectly thet at th' time they looked th' same way t' him.

For several moments after the conclusion of Mr. Abbott's yarn no one spoke.

"Fust hearin' about drinks makes me thirsty this kind of weather," observed Mr. Leary with a slight yawn.

"Me too," admitted the landlord, with a questioning glance at the cigar drummer. " 'Tain't right, Eb to relate things like that in a temperance town."

"Then let's all go up to my room," suggested

Mr. Leary, with an inviting wink. "Come on, Mr. Norton; you're not goin' to leave us this early, are you?"

"Much obliged," the editor declined, "but we go to press tomorrow, and I want to see the staff about some changes on the front page."

This was the most transparent sort of an excuse, for everybody knew that by that time the staff was home with its widowed mother, four miles out in the country.

The Third Skein

"Well, I bagged the last one on my list today," remarked the cigar drummer with satisfaction. "So I'm afraid I'll have to be off in the mornin'."

"You'll be back in the fall, though," the landlord consoled him.

"Oh, certainly. You can't lose Lochinvar Leary while there's a Mansion House in Oxendale."

"Too bad you won't be here for the Circus," said Mr. Sinclair.

"It is hard luck," the drummer agreed. "I haven't been to a really good circus since I was a boy. I stayed over in Porkonia Kan., once, just to see one, but at the last minute the performance fell through *and ended up in a football game. 'Twas almost as good as a circus at that."*

His audience scented narrative and settled expectantly back in their chairs with feet and legs comfortably disposed. When they were ready Mr. Leary started off on—

The Yarn of Football Fantastic

O WING to a careless oversight on the part of the manager of the Porkonia fair grounds, Benson Brothers' Mammoth Circus and Professor Sharpe's Travelin' Wonderland had both been booked for the same day. To make matters worse, the advance agents of both shows struck town on the same train.

"I'm sorry, gentlemen," said the manager when he had explained the way matters stood. "I don't see what we can do about it, though, unless one of you consents to withdraw."

"That would be all right—if the Wonderland people are willin'," spoke up the Circus man.

"If the Wonderland people are willin'?" exclaimed Professor Sharpe's representative. "I trust you don't for a moment imagine that we'd consent to deprive the people of this educational treat that they've been lookin' forward to for—No, sir! Let the Circus people withdraw."

"Tut, tut!" said the Circus man. "Think of the disappointment of the little ones. Besides, if education is what the people want, give it to 'em at the Circus; give it to 'em on a large scale. A little education is a dangerous thing."

"Gentlemen, gentlemen," said the fair grounds manager, "if you'll only listen a moment, I believe I have a solution of this problem which will be equally agreeable to (with a low bow to the Circus agent) your highly educational Circus, and, sir (with a low bow to the Wonderland man), to your most instructive Wonderland."

"Why not settle this dispute with a game of football between your respective greatest shows on earth? Such a contest would draw more than double the crowd that either show could draw alone. And as I have been the cause of this slight misunderstandin', it is only just that I should bear the expense of all advertisin'. Is it a go, gentlemen?"

It was a go. Next day every available fence and barn in the county bore a gaudy four-sheet poster announcin':

Fair Grounds, June 31

2 p.m.

FOOTBALL

Championship of the Universe!!
Benson Bros.' Mammoth Circus

vs.

Prof. Sharpe's Travelin' Wonderland

22

Peerless Performers will Positively Appear

22—Count Them—22

Admission Twenty-five Cents

Well, sir, you never saw such a crowd in all your life as assembled to see that game.

Imagine thousands upon thousands of fat people packed together just as close as you can pack 'em. Then drop thin people into all the chinks where the fat ones don't quite touch—and you've got a pretty good idea of the way the fair grounds looked from the tree where I sat.

There was nothin' remarkable about the first part of the game except the fact that the Wonderlands' guards, the Brothers Jones, said to be the stoutest gentlemen in the world, were forced to play their positions sideways.

You see, if they were to face their opponents, either their corporations would have lapped over so as to put them off the side, or else they would have had to stand so far back as to make more men behind the line than the rules allow.

In spite of this slight handicap, however, play was about even, and the first half ended without either side scorin'.

'Twas along about the middle of the second half that the teams began to show what they had up their sleeves.

The first sensation was when the Human Kangaroo, left half-back for the Circus, hurdled the line with a six-foot leap and tore off fifteen yards before the Wonderlands' Elastic-Skinned full-back brought him to the ground.

He followed this up with a leap for ten yards, but on the third play he found the Wonderlands ready for him. Just as he jumped, they jumped, too, and the Kangaroo was brought to bay for a loss of three yards.

Next time the tables were again turned. Again the Kangaroo made a noble leap. Once more the Wonderlands stooped for their counter leap. But just as they were about to spring, every man of them stopped short with a groan. Their opponents were standing on their toes. The Human Kangaroo lit in the full-back's arms, six yards back of them.

'Twas the Circus's ball on Wonderland's ten-yard line, third down, two yards to gain.

The Wonderlands' captain asked for time out, and gathered his men about him for a conference. Before returnin' to their places it was noticed that each man stooped as though to fix his shoes.

When play was resumed the Kangaroo was once more called upon for one of his remarkable leaps.

Again the Wonderlands stooped to spring in front of him, and this time they shot high in the air, flingin' the runner back for a heavy loss.

The Circus's rushers stared at their feet as though dazed. And well they might. They were standin' on a long line of vacant footwear. The Wonderlands, havin' loosened their laces, had literally jumped out of their shoes.

"Our ball, first down," cried the Wonderland captain, clappin' his hands together briskly. "Here, there, you backs. Get up in the line and change places with the Brothers Ayre. Now then boys, get at 'em, hard and low!"

"Fourteen—six—thirty-eight—Y," sang out the quarterback.

The two smaller of the Brothers Ayre leaped lightly to the third brother's shoulders, and a moment later stood one upon the other in their wonderful human Eiffel Tower act.

"Seventeen—X Y Z—eleven," continued the

"Seventeen—X Y Z—eleven," continued the quarter-back.

The Turtle Boy snapped the ball back to the quarter, who in turn passed it up to the topmost Ayre.

Just as the Circus line was breakin' through, the human tower toppled gracefully forward, thereby gainin' its length, a good five yards.

The human Eiffel Tower act proved invincible for a time. The Brothers Ayre toppled off five yards at a tumble until it was Wonderland's first down on their opponent's 25-yard line.

The Benson Brothers were ragin' up and down the side lines, wavin' their arms like wild men.

Finally, in despair, they ordered the whole Circus team, Human Kangaroo and all, off the field, and substituted their eleven invincible Cossack tumblers.

"If a Cossack pyramid can't stop that fallin' tower," they growled, "nothin' on this earth can."

"Sixteen—P D Q—eleven—A," the Wonderland quarter called.

The Brothers Ayre nimbly mounted into their tower formation. At the same time, there was a

Lochinvar Leary, the Cigar Drummer, and
Ezra Norton, Editor of the Oxendale *Townsman*.

general scramblin' among the Cossacks, and a moment later the human Eiffel Tower was facin' a grimly determined pyramid of equal height.

"Thirteen—fifty-two," concluded the quarter-back. The two human eminences toppled over against each other with a crash that caused a mass of spectators to seethe with enthusiasm.

"But where's the ball?" people began to ask each other. "The topmost Ayre didn't get it."

No. The quarter-back, forseein' what would happen, had passed the ball to the Elastic-Skinned Man, and that worthy had cleared the left end just in time to escape the shower of players from the towers above.

The apex of the pyramid espied him first. With a howl of rage he disentangled himself from the groanin' debris and gave pursuit.

He was swift as a deer, and as the 10-yard line made a long, low dive and caught the runner by the calf.

But the Elastic-Skinned Man was under full headway, and stretched a good three yards beyond the spot where the Cossack held his calf. Then, suddenly jumpin' from the ground, he snapped back with a force that knocked his captor senseless. The next instant he was scamperin' over the line for the touchdown that finally won the game for Wonderland.

The Travelin' Wonderland's tattooed man can prove all this. He has the score upon his chest.

"Well, I'll be hanged!" exclaimed Mr. Sinclair, slapping his knee. "Then that's the show the Human Louvre was with before he joined us. I always wondered what '6—0' just below the Chinese dragon on his chest meant. Don't it beat all how small this world is!"

Mr. Leary regarded the Circus man intently for a few moments, and then, with a deep sigh, silently passed him over a cigar.

"Football's a durn dangerous game," commented Mr. Abbott authoritatively. "Young Will Cole had his leg broke all on account uv football."

"Why," interposed Mr. Norton, with considerable surprise, "I always understood that young Cole's leg was broken in a trolley car accident."

"*Wal, anyway, he was probably on his way to a football game when it happened,*" persisted the Sage of Oxendale. "*He'd've been all right if he'd stayed t' home.*"

"*I never saw football,*" observed the landlord, who had been gazing thoughtfully at the ceiling, "*but I've often thought that it must be a very interesting game. When I played baseball on the famous Lightfoot Lilies, who used to hold the championship of Jones County—*"

"*You don't mean to say that* you *ever played baseball!*" exclaimed the Circus man, surveying the landlord's 360 pounds incredulously.

Mr. Little flushed.

"*Not only did I play, sir, but, if I do say it myself, I had few equals on the diamond before I grew too stout to touch the bag when sliding bases on my stomach.*

"*But as I was about to remark, when I played on the famous Lightfoot Lilies, we had a catcher that I think would have made a mighty good football-player. He was the strongest man I ever laid eyes on. And, unlike the ordinary Circus strong*

man, he combined his brawn with brains."
Continuing, the landlord unwound—

The Yarn of the Brawny Batsman

I can see Bull Thompson as if he were standing behind the plate now. As the batter would face the pitcher, the Bull would straighten up and draw in his breath until he was red in the face.

Then, pop! would go the top button off his shirt, and while the batter was rubbing the back of his neck and wondering what in Jones County had struck him, Dean Braley, our pitcher, would shoot the ball over for as pretty a strike as ever split the plate. Some chest expansion had big Bull Thompson.

And bat? Why, say, that man used to hit so everlasting far, that if the people over the State line hadn't been jealous of our nine, they'd have made our opponents take out extradition papers before they'd let 'em field the ball back.

But the Bull's slugging wasn't as advantageous to the Lilies as you might suppose. He soon acquired such a reputation with teams throughout that part of the country that the instant the batsman preceding him had been disposed of, the outfielders would take it on the run for the furthermost ruffles on the outskirts of the city. In that way, with a slow pitcher and good start, they were just as apt as not to get there in time to nab the Bull's hits.

Sometimes the Bull tried to vary his herculean swipes with an occasional well-placed bunt to centerfield. Such restraint of muscle, however, was little to his liking, and he sought for other means to baffle the fielders who used to stand waist deep in the horizon awaiting his long ones.

At last he solved the problem. Instead of driving the ball out over the diamond, he hit upon the plan of swinging his bat down on it and driving it onto the home plate.

When he did this, the ball, under the impetus of his mighty blow, would rebound from the plate to such a height that before it came to earth again he'd have ample time to reach first base and sometimes even second.

There was a stunt for you! They couldn't field

him out, because the ball was in the air, and they couldn't hope to catch him out because it had got there on first bounce.

I'll never as long as I live forget the way he foxed the redoubtable Ringtail Roarers with that stunt.

A mean, drizzling rain that had been falling all morning made the diamond soggy and slow when the big game was called, but the thousands that had driven in from every corner of the State put postponement out of the question.

The first time at bat, the Bull let drive for one of his long ones over center. Old Doc Quackenbush, who was umpiring, trained his field-glasses on it and finally diagnosed the runner out, twenty-six seconds after the ball had left his bat.

In the fourth, with Slugger Burrows, the Lily captain, on third, the Bull resorted to his new trick and basted the ball down against the plate with a force that bounced it high enough to enable the Slugger to score.

In the seventh, a similar plate bounder, only higher, brought in two runs.

The Roarers' outfielders were still playing deep,

as there was no telling when the Bull would take it into his head to shift tactics and wallop out one of his long shots.

In fact, it took them so long to get in from their positions after the Bull had been at bat that the game was delayed considerably.

When Bull Thompson came to bat in the last half of the ninth you could have heard a snowflake fall. The score stood 6—3 in favor of the Roarers, the Lilies had the bases full, and two were out.

What would the Bull do? Driving the ball against the plate for a 50-foot bounce was sure to be good for a hit, but that would only bring in two men at the most, which would leave the Roarers still one run to the good, and Jim Timpson, the next man up, was almost a sure out.

On the other hand, the Roarers' fielders were back beyond the town limits waiting expectantly for one of the Bull's long ones. What would the Bull do?

Cy Priest, the Roarers' pitcher, drew his arm back, and a second later the ball was sailing square over the plate.

Down whizzed the Bull's bat on it like a maternal slipper descending upon a wayward son, and—whack!

The Bull was off like a flash for first and the man on third was tearing home.

The Roarers rushed toward the plate to gather in the ball on its descent.

"Where is it? Who sees it?" shouted Cy Priest, peering anxiously skyward.

The runner on third dashed across the plate.

"There it is! There it is!" cried the Roarers' catcher, dancing up and down and pointing excitedly.

"Where? Where? Pshaw! That's only a bird!"

A second fleeting Lily crossed the plate.

"Where in thunder's that ball? Don't any one see it?" roared Priest, shading his eyes with his hands and gazing intently into the heavens.

The third Lily crossed the plate, and the score was tied.

By this time all the men, women and children were on their feet with heads back, scanning the clouds for sign or sight of Thompson's hit.

A moment later a mighty roar shook the stands,

and the crowds began pouring out onto the field. Bull Thompson had completed the circuit with the winning run.

"Give us room, give us room," said Cy Priest, motioning the crowd back. "I'm going to stay here until that ball comes down. I don't believe he hit the darn thing at all."

The Bull merely shrugged his shoulders in an injured sort of way and gave the crowd one of those comical winks of his.

Well, sir, those Ringtail Roarers must have gawked 'round there gazing up in the air for half an hour or more before Cy Priest finally gave the thing up as a bad job and happened to glance down at his feet.

"Simplicity Jefferson!" he exlaimed with a start.

There, not more than half a foot in front of the home plate, was a perfectly round hole about three inches in diameter.

Yes, sir, you've guessed it. Instead of swatting that ball against the hard plate where 'twould have bounded back up in the air, he'd pasted it down onto the soggy earth so hard that he'd driven it over two feet into the ground. We got it out with a pick next morning.

Playing yet? No, the Bull got all bunged up in a runaway eight years ago and had to quit the game. Yanked the horses back with such a jerk that he pulled 'em clean over on top of him. Leg, both arms, three ribs and a collarbone busted.

Last I heard of him he was down in Chihuahua making wigs for those Mexican hairless dogs.

"Baseball's certainly a fine game," conceded the Circus man. "It's all on the level. You can't tell who's going to win until the last man's out. There's nothing crooked in it like there is in horse-racing. Why, what show does an outsider like us stand playing the races?"

"None at all," declared the editor.

"Unless—," the cigar drummer started to suggest.

"Unless what?"

"Oh, well, there's probably nothin' in it, but several years ago when I was bein' shown through the Porkonia (Kan.) Insane Asylum, one of the inmates told me of a system he had for beatin' the races that rather impressed me at the time. I'll give

*it to you the way he gave it to me, and you can judge
for yourselves.*

The Yarn of the Certain
System

HIS HIGH, scholarly brow, and deep-set, intelligent eyes at once placed him above the ordinary inmates.

"What's he in here for?" I inquired of the keeper.

"Ask him. He's harmless."

I did. For a moment he closely scrutinized me. "You seem like a man of education and understandin'," he finally observed without the slightest trace of insanity. "And since the fickleness of fortune renders my great secret useless to me, I know of no reason why I should not share it with you. In fact, if you were to take a billion or two dollars from my enemies it would to some slight extent revenge my wrongs."

His eyes fired with enthusiasm at the thought of it.

"I," he whispered dramatically, "am the author

of the only certain system to beat the races that has ever been devised. That," he added with a deep sigh, "is why I am where you see me now. I was betrayed by a supposed friend. The pool-room trust got wind of my wonderful scheme, and, in order to avert the absolute ruin they saw impendin', had me railroaded into this insane asylum.

"What is this wonderful system? Listen:

"For the sake of convenience, let us assume that we are now in New York. As you undoubtedly know, there is a difference in time between New York and Chicago of about one hour. That is to say, when it is six o'clock in New York it is only five o'clock in Chicago.

"In the same way, San Francisco is three times as far west as Chicago, so that there is three hours' difference in time. That is, when it is six o'clock in New York it is only three o'clock in San Francisco. Do you follow me?

"The further west we go the greater the difference in time. If we go eight times as far west as San Francisco we naturally gain eight times three hours, or, roughly speakin', a whole day.

"But where is eight times as far west as San Francisco? Why, sir, it's all the way 'round the world and back to New York again."

He paused, and drew back to watch the effect of his remarkable reasonin'.

"In other words," I ventured to suggest, "if you've been 'round the world in the meantime, today is really yesterday?"

"Precisely. But to put it in a more practical way," he continued in an impressive whisper, "if you send yourself a telegram around the world, westward, you'll get it the day before you write it."

"But what's all that got to do with beatin' the races?" I asked.

"Why, don't you see? Take today's list of winners, for example. If I telegraph it to a friend of mine in Chicago, 'twill reach him an hour ago by Chicago time.

"He'll wire it to a friend in San Francisco. 'Twill reach there three hours ago by 'Frisco time. The 'Frisco man will cable it on to a friend in Honolulu, and so on all the way 'round the globe until it reaches me in New York again just twenty-four hours before I've sent it in the first place.

"The minute I receive the telegram I start out to make the rounds of all the poolrooms, and back each winner for all they'll take on him. After that, it's only a matter of sittin' down and waitin' until it's time to cash in.

"You look incredulous. It seems too easy to be true, you think. You wonder how—But, ssh!—the keeper is edgin' toward us. I think he already suspects."

With that he switched the subject and began to talk about the cryin' need of a cattle corset that would cause cows to give condensed milk.

For several moments after the conclusion of Mr. Leary's yarn no one spoke. They were in deep thought. It was the editor of The Townsman *who finally broke the silence:*

"Why, according to your friend's scheme, then—"

"No friend of mine," the drummer cheerily assured him. "That was the only time I ever saw him in my life."

"If this scheme is feasible," persisted the editor,

"I don't see what's to confine it to horse-racing. For example, why couldn't a man who had just died have his obituary notice telegraphed 'round the world to him and get it in time to read it before he passed away?"

"I'm sure I don't know, Mr. Norton. Why couldn't he?" The drummer rose and stretched. "Well, gentlemen, I've got to catch an early train in the mornin', and I think I'd better—"

"Don't go yet," urged the Circus man. "I'm going on that 7:10 myself, but I promised to meet my bill-poster here. He ought to be along 'most any minute now. Wait awhile, and we'll all go up and have a night-cap together."

The cigar drummer yawned, and, with an air of resignation, resumed his seat.

The Fourth Skein

*"By the way, I knew there was something I wanted to ask you and Mr. Sinclair before you left,"
said the landlord as soon as Mr. Leary had comfortably arranged his feet on the stove again.
"When I played baseball on the famous Lightfoot Lilies, our nearest rivals for the championship of Jones County, the Redoubtable Ringtail Roarers, either had or didn't have, a man who undoubtedly was—if there ever was such a man—the fastest runner that ever ran, or didn't run, as the case may have been. I was wondering whether either you or Mr. Sinclair, in the course of your extensive travels, had ever run across him? Wyndham Hare,*

his name was."

Each shook his head in negation.

"At least, I don't recall the name," the Circus man added. "But tell us about him. I may have met him at that—if there ever was such a man, of course."

The landlord waddled over behind the desk and unlocked the safe. After rummaging around a few seconds, he drew out a couple of newspaper clippings, yellow with age.

"It's a very remarkable story," he explained when he had resumed his seat, "and I like to have all the facts at hand."

With this foreword he unwound—

The Yarn of the Fleet-Footed Fielder

THE Lightfoot Lilies first heard of Wyndham Hare in this way: Captain Slugger Burrows and the rest of us were sitting 'round the post-office stove one early spring evening when Bull Thompson suddenly let out a whistle that would have stopped work in a stamp mill.

"Listen to this," he said, pointing to an article in the baseball column of *The Jones County Courier*. I have the article here.

"The Lightfoot Lilies," read the Bull, "will have their hands full defending the county championship this spring. Their ancient rivals, the Ringtail Roarers, have materially strengthened their already formidable aggregation of ball-tossers by the acquisition of a new outfielder, Mr. Wyndham Hare, whom Captain Priest tells us is without doubt the fastest baserunner that ever donned a uniform.

"Captain Priest's attention was first drawn to Mr. Hare under rather remarkable circumstances. While visiting Bloody Gulch, Kansas, he was witness to a street altercation. One of the disputants suddenly pulled a gun and fired. At the same instant the other man turned and fled.

"He was as fleet as the bullet. For five blocks he maintained a slight lead. Then he seemed to weaken a little, and for the next few yards the bullet almost touched his coat.

"Just as he was nearing the end of the sixth block, however, a mighty shout went up from the spectators who had been attracted by the report of the gun, and they crowded around him to extend their congratulations. The bullet had spent its force and lay harmless on the sidewalk, five yards back of the runner.

"Among the first to grasp the hero's hand was Captain Priest. Learning that in addition to his wonderful running Mr. Hare (for Mr. Hare it was) was something of a ball-player, the shrewd Roarer captain signed him on the spot. We expect great things of you, Wyndham Hare."

"Well, now, what do you think of that!" piped up Sammie Salmon when the Bull had finished reading.

"Huh!" sneered Slugger Burrows. "If you believe everything you hear, you'll get a bee in your ear some of these days and think you're the Franco-Prussian war."

But in spite of this, we knew by the tangled thought ditches on his brow that Slugger was sort of worried himself.

We could hardly wait for the frost to get out of the ground before we started practise.

For the next five weeks we scanned *The Courier* regularly. There was no further mention of the wonderful Hare, and we began to have hopes that there might be nothing in the report after all.

But on Friday evening of the sixth week, Sammie Salmon burst into the post-office with the latest edition of *The Courier,* and began to read excitedly. I have it here:

"The Ringtail Roarers," read Sammie, "are being greatly hampered in their daily practice for the big match with the Lightfoot Lilies by the fleetness of foot of their lately acquired phenomenon, Wyndham Hare. We have it from no less authority than Captain Cy Priest himself, that Hare raises so much dust when he skirts the bases that it is fully fifteen minutes before the diamond settles sufficiently for play to proceed. In spite of the loss of practice thus occasioned, however, the Roarers are confident of pulling up the Lilies by their roots when the proper time comes."

Well, sir, as you can imagine, that little item sort of put a damper on things, and set each man to thinking pretty hard on his way home that night.

The thing that capped the climax, though, was a letter that Slugger got from Cy Priest the week before the game.

"My dear Burrows," Priest wrote, "you have undoubtedly seen mentioned in the public prints of the incredible speed of our new outfielder, Wyndham Hare. The reports of his raising so much dust that we have to wait fifteen minutes for the diamond to settle before resuming play err only on the side of conservatism. Therefore, knowing that you are the last man to wish our contest next Saturday to terminate prematurely on account of darkness, I appeal to you to have the base-line macadamized and to make arrangements with the town watering-cart to sprinkle the grounds between innings. Should this plan meet with your approval, as I feel sure it will, the Ringtail Roarers will gladly bear half the expense thus incurred.

"Yours for the welfare of the national game,— Cyrus Priest."

"Of course you'll do it," ventured Sammie Salmon.

"Of course I won't," said Slugger. "If this Windy Hare guy raises such dustclouds that the base-line gets up in the air, why, let him go ahead and do it. Unless the next man up can fly, I'll have him declared out for running out of base-line. Do you think I'm going to have Lily Park all torn up and lose the last week of practise just to please Cy Priest?

It was with anything but confidence that we trotted on the field the day of the big contest.

"Say, Cap," whispered Salmon, "if he hits the ball at all, I suppose we'd best field right to the plate. There wouldn't be any hope of getting it to third ahead of him, would there?"

"Play the game as you always play it," growled Slugger.

When the Roarers came out for preliminary practise, there was a great craning of necks to see which was the wonderful Hare. The only new face on the team was the left-fielder.

Slugger Burrows won the toss, and took the field. The stranger went to bat first for the Roarers.

On the second ball pitched he tapped a little grounder to Dean Braley, and although the Dean was a bit rattled like the rest of us, he shot the ball over in plenty of time to catch the runner at first.

"Was he really out?" asked Sammie Salmon in astonishment. "Or was that his second time around?"

"Second time 'round nothing!" shouted Slugger. "Why, that guy couldn't beat a steam-roller going the other way."

He certainly wasn't anything to inspire an express-train with jealousy.

The Lilies began to recover their nerve, and as the game progressed, they gradually forged ahead.

Cy Priest, who was sore in the first place at the failure of his ruse to deprive the Lilies of their practise by getting them to tear up their grounds, grew grouchier and grouchier with every minute of play.

In the ninth, when the Roarers' leftfielder was caught napping off second, leaving the final score 13 to 7 in favor of the Lilies, Priest's face was the picture of pickled disappointment.

"Say, Cy, what was the matter with that famous Hare of yours?" Slugger jeered. "Sort of all tangled up today, wasn't he?"

Priest glared at Slugger.

"I hope you didn't think that stiff was Wyndham Hare, did you?" he asked with a sneer. "Why, Hare's in the hospital. Sprained his back in a game last week. Knocked a home run, and ran 'round the bases so fast that he caught up with himself and collided."

That's only what Cy Priest said, of course. Personally, I don't believe it.

"Neither do I," grunted Mr. Abbott.

"It seems to me," the editor insinuatingly observed, "that I remember reading that story in a newspaper somewheres."

"I don't doubt it," said the landlord, not the least bit ruffled.

"It all came out in the sporting page of The Jones County Courier *at the time."*

Before the editor could reply, a sad-eyed man with unshorn locks and bushy brows appeared at the door.

"Oh, hello Lorraine," the Circus man greeted him. "Come in. I've bee: waiting for you. What luck!"

The sad-eyed one struck an attitude and cleared his throat.

"I have posted Oxendale," he announced in sep-

ulchral tones; "I have posted North Oxendale, Oxendale Center, West Oxendale,—yea, and even Oxendale Junction have I posted. Neither barn nor fence hath escaped my hand. Tomorrow, fate willing, I will on to Bullardvale."

"Good," said the Circus Man. "But wait a second, will you? I'd better get you a copy of my itinerary so you'll know where to find me if anything goes wrong. I've got one in my room."

The landlord motioned to the chair the Circus man had just vacated.

"Pray be seated, sir."

"Bill-poster, eh?" inquired Mr. Abbott. "Humph. Thet's funny. I'd've picked ye out fur a play-actor every time."

"For many years I did follow the Profession," explained the newcomer. "But gradually, through force of circumstances, I drifted away from the draymatic art over to the pictorial so that today, sir, I am, as you have correctly divined, a bill-poster —nothing but a common bill-poster. Ah, gentlemen, as the gentle Bard of Avon so aptly hath it,"—here Mr. Lorraine made a dramatic gesture ceilingward, *and huskily demanded:*

> *"O mighty Caesar! Dost thou lie so low?*
> *Are all thy conquests, glories, triumphs, spoils,*
> *Shrunk to this little measure?"*

"Any one can see that you're still an actor at heart," the drummer kindly assured him. "What difference does it make that you're no longer on the stage? To the true artist, 'all the world's a stage?' "

"A truer word ne'er passed the lips of our immortal Will," the ex-Thespian agreed. "Of all the parts I've acted, those which I've acted off the boards in the great drayma of every-day life have been the best. You've never seen me on the stage? Ah, then you cannot realize the startling nature of my statement."

The Yarn of the Thespian Triumphant

WHY, out in Bleeding Heart, Mont., when night after night I thrilled thousands upon thousands with my masterly *Richard III*, my acting was so realistic as to actually endanger the life of one of my fellow players. The realism of my death scene was such as to cause the audience to rise to their feet with cries of vengeance for the luckless *Richmond.*

"Lynch him! Lynch him! Kill the other one, too!" they shouted.

My great "Romeo and Juliet" triumph took place in Wisconsin the same year. So lifelike was my death scene that the audience could not be persuaded that I still lived. In spite of the manager's protest, they demanded that the curtain be rung down as a matter of respect. The local paper next morning, still under the impression that my death was genuine, paid me a touching tribute. Under the heading "A Dead One," it spoke of me as "an awful loss as *Romeo.*"

But, as I remarked in the first place, my most

finished bits of art have been those enacted on the stage of every-day life.

For example, there was the time I laid the ghosts in Broken Skull, Kansas. A man had bought a farmhouse. He was a stranger to the country and thought he'd struck a bargain.

But he soon found out that the place was dear at any price. Men would not work on it, the crops would not grow, the cattle sickened and died. Strange sounds at night, such as the clanking of chains and the breaking of glass, made the place unbearable. In short, the house was haunted.

The man was about to give the place up in despair when luckily he heard of me. You'll scarcely believe what I tell you unless you've seen me act, but after I'd given two performances as *Hamlet's Ghost*, every other shade on the premises, green with envy, melted away and has never been seen since. Today there isn't a more fertile farm for miles around.

But my crowning achievement was the time I saved the Deadwood coach. You've never heard of it? Alas, such is earthly fame!

We had just reached a lonely place in the road when a troop of masked horsemen dashed out of the impenetrable forest that lined either side of the pass.

"Halt!" their leader cried in stentorian tones.

As we were all unarmed, there was nothing else to do.

"Dismount! Up with your hands!" commanded Jesse James, for it was none other than the intrepid James himself.

Again we obeyed.

'Twas at this point that my mastery of the draymatic art saved the day.

Quickly changing from the attitude of abject terror which I had purposely assumed on first alighting from the coach, I took upon an expression of unspeakable relief and joy.

"They come!" I cried, pointing down the road with one hand, and snapping the fingers of the other in a life-like imitation of galloping horses. "They come! We are saved!"

The robbers, completely taken in by my ruse, turned to look. As they did so, I threw stones down

Mr. Lorraine, the Bill Poster and ex Play-actor, and
Mr. D'Arcy Sinclair, of Ring Brothers' Stupendous Circus.

the road, still snapping my fingers like clattering hoofs. Great dust-clouds arose where the stones struck. The robbers, thoroughly terrified at the approach of the rescuing party, as they supposed, threw themselves into their saddles and galloped off as fast as spur-driven horses could carry them.

"Oh, beg pardon, sir, I didn't hear you come in, sir," stammered the bill-poster in confusion, as he turned and saw the Circus man quietly regarding him with an amused smile.

"That's all right. I've been enjoying your reminiscences immensely. Here's my itinerary up till Saturday." The Circus man handed him a list.

"Yes, sir. Yes, sir. I bid you a pleasant evening, gentlemen." And the Thespian bill-poster made a hurried exit.

"D'ye s'pose thet all he wus tellin' us really happended?" asked Mr. Abbott when he had gone. "Or is it jest somethin' he's heard when he wus talkin' to himself?"

"Oh, he's not so bad," spoke up the Circus man. "Lorraine's honest, and that's more than you can

say about a good many men. He's had some pretty tough rows to hoe in his time, but in spite of all the bumps and knocks, he's stayed as straight as the day is long."

"And why wouldn't he stay straight?" demanded the sage. "It's a matter of policy, honesty is. He don't deserve any credit fur thet. It pays t' be good. Virtue beats vice in every race, an', in addition t' bein' it's own reward, it usually pulls in a few of the outside bets of life along with it.

"I know of a case thet happened right here in Oxendale. I won't mention the young feller's name, 'cause ye'd know him in a minute if I did, an' his folks are hardworkin', respectable people. We'll call him Jake, jest because thet warn't his name, nor anything like it."

The Yarn of the Sinner Stung

JAKE wus a bad man clean through. He drank an' he cussed, an' Lor' knows what he didn't do. He'd steal the dinner-bag off'n a blind horse if he thought there wus oats in it.

As fur me, on the other hand, I've always lived a good Christian life an' never done no crittur harm, as any one who ever knew me'll tell ye. I knew Jake's old man, an' felt sorry to see th' boy goin' wrong. Why, I've talked t' him with tears in my eyes as big as horse-chestnuts, tryin' t' get him t' change his ways an' walk the path of righteousness. Little good it did, though, as you'll see.

'Twus on as likely a spring Sunday as ye ever saw thet Jake met his end. We wus walkin' through th' woods leadin' t' Morton's Drop. Everything wus peaceable. Th' bees wus buzzin' 'round th' wild flowers along th' path an' th' little birds wus a-titterin' in th' trees, all so joyful-like, thet it seemed it oughter soften any man's heart.

I pleaded with Jake durin' thet walk as I'd never pleaded before. By th' time I'd finished talkin' we'd reached th' end of th' path an' stood on th' edge of th' precipice, a-lookin' down on the calm lake thet lies below.

Suddenly Jake wheeled around facin' me. A strange look came into his eyes an' I drew back skeered-like.

"Gol durn you, Ebenezer Abbott," he growled. "What th' 'ell right have you t' be talkin t' me th' way y' have, y' old varmint, ye? I've half a mind t' heave ye off inter—"

With that he sprung at me like a wildcat.

"Help!" I hollered, but he grabbed hold of my throat and shut me off.

There we fought like two hyenas, he a-tryin' t' throw me off, an' me a-tryin' not t' let him.

Back an' forth we swayed. But he was younger'n I wus, and finally his strength began t' tell. He gave one final push an' over I went. But I made a desprit clutch at his coat, an' he came, too.

Down, down, down!

Poor Jake met a just but awful death in th' placid lake below.

"But how did you get out of it?" asked the drummer. "You went down with him."

"Me? Oh, jest as we struck th' water I woke up and found 'twus nothin' but a dream with me. But poor Jake, he never woke up. All of which goes t' show th' truth of what I said about—" the rest was lost in a wide yawn.

THE END